I0674630

SHARDS OF SHADOW BOOK 1

A TRAITOR IN THE SHADOWS

JOSEPH R. LALLO

Published by:

Heart Ally Books, LLC
heartallybooks.com
26910 92nd Ave NW C5-406, Stanwood, WA 98292
Published on Camano Island, WA, USA

ISBN-13: 978-0-9997081-8-7 (paperback)

10 9 8 7 6 5 4 3 2 1

CONTENTS

CHAPTER 1

The sun was low in the sky. Shadows stretched across the road, cast by the hulking behemoths of tractor-trailers and logging trucks. Alan grinned. For a lot of people, having the sun eclipsed by a truck that could crush their little compact coupe without even noticing would be harrowing. For him, it was nostalgic. Once a year, for as long as he could remember, he watched these same road markers whisk by. As the cities began to thin out and snowy farms started to flank the highway, he knew he was getting close to his destination. "The land." Back then he could only sit in the back seat, crammed between his brother and sister, and listen to one of the six albums his father had. Now he was the one behind the wheel. He was alone with the road. It was meditative. Peaceful.

On cue, his ringing phone shattered the magical moment.

He grumbled a bit. His car was new enough that he could answer the phone with the tap of a button on his steering wheel. At least that meant he wouldn't have to miss the call. He pressed it, and the instrumental he'd been listening to was replaced with the almost-silence of a cell phone call.

"Hi, Mom. Hang on," he said. "I'll pull over."

"You don't have to pull over, Alan. You have a hands-free, don't you?" She seldom wasted time with a hello if she could use that precious breath on gentle nags.

"Distracted driving is as bad as drunk driving," Alan said simply.

"You should be there by now, shouldn't you?"

"Not according to Google." He pulled off to the shoulder and put it in park. "And not if people keep calling me."

"Your father always beats Google."

"Dad also treats the speed limit as a minimum instead of a maximum."

"And it's always worked fine for him."

"How many speeding tickets has he gotten this year, Mom?"

"Oh, who keeps count of those kinds of things?"

"The police do, Mom. But what's up?"

"Did you hit the land yet?"

"Not yet. Close though. I just drove past the tractor supply place."

"I can't believe that place is still open."

He sighed. "It isn't. It had a for sale sign on it."

"Oh... I guess change reaches all the way to the country, huh?"

"Yeah."

"Well, I don't want to keep you. I just wanted to let you know that we just got the last call from the lawyer. The price is set. The place is pretty much sold. It's all over but some legal stuff and the signing."

Alan sagged a bit. "I see. That's good," he said in a tone that failed miserably to match the sentiment.

"It was the right thing to do, Alan," she said. "The family can't afford the taxes on the place, and lord knows we could all use the money."

"I know. But, you know. It wouldn't have broken my heart if the deal had fallen through again. I'm going to miss this place. But at least that solves your money problems, right?"

"Depends on how you look at it," she said.

She sounded almost sheepish. Alan's jaw tightened.

"I'm looking at it as 'now you're not in debt anymore.' How are you looking at it?"

"Don't get mad."

"When has that phrase ever worked, Mom? What's up?"

"It's nothing. I don't want to worry you."

A truck drove by, rattling his little car with the wind alone.

"I'd rather be worried about something that's really happening than worry about what I think might be happening."

"It's just another credit card. That's all."

"How much, Mom?"

"Who keeps track of those sorts of things?"

"*The bank, Mom.* How much?"

"I think it was twelve thousand."

His fists creaked around the vinyl-wrapped steering wheel. "How do you forget you have a credit card with a twelve-thousand-dollar balance?"

"It didn't have twelve thousand dollars when I forgot about it."

He pinched the bridge of his nose. "Yeah, that's how interest works, Mom."

"Don't get fresh."

"Sorry." Another truck rattled his car. "So what's this mean?"

"We'll be fine. We can probably pay it down a little with what's left from the money for the land. The rest we'll chip away at like always."

"Do you need anything? I can probably help you out with a couple hundred—"

"Don't lie to your mother. I talked to your sister. She told me all about how the gallery show did."

He narrowed his eyes. "She did, did she?" he said flatly.

"Don't worry about us. Enjoy your solar eclipse."

"Lunar eclipse, Mom. And thanks, I will. Love you."

"Love you too. Buh-bye."

"Talk to you later."

She hung up and the strings and horns of an old film score faded back to replace the call.

"Sarah had to bring up the gallery show, didn't she?" he muttered, easing the car back up to speed.

Between the snow ditch on one side and the barreling trucks on the other side, it was no small feat getting his little econobox of a car up to highway speeds without wiping out spectacularly. Sometimes being safe was just as dangerous as the alternative.

Once he merged onto the highway again and watched familiar wobbly old barns ease by, he felt the irritation and anxiety of the call and the traffic maneuvers ease away.

"There's the slanty shanty," he murmured with a grin.

A dilapidated barn appeared from behind a white hill that in the summer would be sporting the stalks of yet another cornfield. The rickety wooden structure had been crooked and on the verge of collapse for as long as he could remember. Most of the slats were missing. The darn thing was skewed almost 45 degrees, but it stubbornly refused to fall.

He took a breath and signaled an upcoming turn onto the unpaved road that would lead to the land.

"This'll be good. A fitting goodbye. This is where I saw my first eclipse ever. This is where I got interested in photography. Seems right that the last thing I do is get some great shots of another lunar eclipse." His smile widened. "I wonder if that old, dead Dutch elm is still standing. I bet that'd be *perfect*..."

His tires crunched over some icy gravel as he passed the real estate sign. A chain with some orange flags tied to it separated the land from the road. It was a bit pointless. No one ever came up this road, and even if some criminals came this way with nefarious deeds in mind, there wasn't anything left on the land but trees and rocky soil. If someone *were* dead set on stealing the old mossy rock by the creek, chances were good a chain between two rotten fence posts wouldn't turn them away.

He unlocked the chain and threw it aside, then drove his car into the snow-scattered field. It was mid-November. Normally, this time of year the snow would be higher than his tires. They'd always treated this more as a summer camp and left it for the deer in the winter, which was probably why it was agreed that the family couldn't afford it anymore. Good fortune or the ravages of global warming had left it with just a sprinkle of snow for this final visit. The inch or two of fresh powder were just enough to leave the countryside looking clean and new. A spectacular backdrop for a photo.

Alan pulled his car over to the fence and stepped out of the car. He'd gotten far too many two-wheel-drive cars mired in this field to risk taking it any farther. He took a deep breath and watched it curl from his lips as cool fog.

One thing that no one had questioned about the land was how they'd afforded it in the first place. The weird little strip of land was a few dozen acres that had been sliced off a much larger, much better bit of farmland. The only road access for this piece was the dirt road behind him. A slow-moving creek made most of the northeast corner of the land a mosquito-infested bog in the warmer months. It seemed like you couldn't dig more than a few inches without hitting enough rocks to make you rethink the whole idea of digging in the first place. Basically, the only redeeming quality of the place was that it wasn't the city.

And that was exactly what convinced his parents and their siblings they should buy it.

He popped open the hatchback and slid a beat-up but serviceable hiking pack onto his shoulders. A much sturdier and more professional camera bag came next. He zipped it open to reveal a staggering assortment of photography equipment: two different camera bodies, both with the rubber gaskets indicative of the pricier weather-resistant models; half a dozen lenses; remote shutters; pan-and-tilt mechanisms. The contents of the bag cost more than the car that carried them.

Alan assembled a photographic configuration with the speed and efficiency of an assassin prepping his rifle in a cheesy action movie. He swiped a microfiber cloth across the UV filter on his camera and snapped a batch of photos.

"Fantastic," he crowed, clicking through the previews.

As tended to be the case, he found his mind doing the sort of freelance arithmetic that was necessary to keep the overdraft fees to a minimum these days. This image would work perfectly for a tourism board's brochures. That shot would look great with a motivational slogan and framed at some cubicle-strewn office. These three would probably get him a couple of bucks if he sold them to a stock photo service.

He shook himself. Of all the side effects of having to hustle like mad to keep his rent paid, this was the one that bothered him the most. He *loved* photography. Composing pictures, finding new and interesting things to take snaps of, these were the things that drove him. Strangely, as soon as he started to work out how to put a price on his photos, they started to feel so much cheaper.

It didn't help that selling his art hadn't even been all that profitable. As he clicked back through the previous images, he quickly reached shots of a museum event, then a red-carpet thing in Manhattan. The memory card was stuffed with candid shots of celebrities getting off planes, getting into limos, and generally trying to shield their faces. The worst of them fetched ten times what a beautiful landscape would, even before he'd signed up with an outfit that could presell them and give him assignments. And yet, even debasing himself with the work of a paparazzi hadn't been enough to keep this hunk of land in the family.

He raised the camera to take one more shot. "And that one's for my wall." He clicked on the lens cover, secured the camera bag, and slammed the hatchback. "Okay. Time to find the perfect spot."

He huffed and puffed as he crested a hill. This place was astounding. For one, he wasn't sure how something that wasn't much larger than a city park back home could give him the feeling he was hiking in the wilderness. For another, despite him spending months here over the course of several years, it managed to look completely different during the winter than it did during the summer. He'd almost given up hope on finding the spot he had in mind after trekking about until the sun slipped behind the mountains.

Finally, he saw the ragged, broken branches of a long-dead tree, and a smile lit up his face.

"There it is! The Gnarly Tree!"

He resisted the urge to run up to the tree and inspect it. It was perched all by itself on the top of a small hill, and the snow around it was pristine and untouched. While it would be neat to see if the stuff he'd carved into it was still there, the visual of a craggy gray tree rising up out of flawless white snow was too good to wreck with his own footprints.

"Look at you. Tonight's your big night."

Like so many things about this little trip, the tree seemed quite literally picture perfect for what he had in mind. A victim of Dutch elm disease, the tree had died long ago. Decades of harsh winters had sculpted it into nothing short of a work of art. Like the barn he'd passed along the way, it was downright miraculous that it had yet to collapse into a pile of splinters already. A once lush set of branches had been whittled down to two main branches. The smaller ones were snapped off and smoothed away. What remained looked uncannily like a pair of hands reaching up to gather up a scoop of the sky.

Alan set about pitching his raggedy single-person tent. He barely used it these days, but he kept it around because it was easy to set up, kept him relatively dry, and as such was indispensable on his rare but beloved photography weekends to the wilderness. Inside of twenty minutes, he had the tent all set up, and then it was time to start the far more important task of setting up the camera.

He'd had this in mind for the last two years, ever since he'd learned a total lunar eclipse would be crossing over the land. It seemed like fate had smiled on him when the sale of the land had been delayed enough to leave it technically still in the family's name on the day of the eclipse. He pulled out his phone and started to check every aspect he could determine. The moon would rise in about an hour and twenty minutes. The sky was perfectly clear, and the satellite map seemed to imply it would remain so. That was good. He found the spot where, if his figuring was correct, the moon would rise behind the tree. Astronomy maps, a sophisticated compass, and something far closer to trigonometry than he was comfortable doing eventually resolved to a specific point to put his tripod.

Then came the computer programming part of the evening. He loaded up his pan-and-tilt head for the tripod and mounted the camera, each hooked up to a weather-resistant battery pack. More trigonometry worked out the exact arc the moon would follow, and the exact timing of its path. There was software to handle all that, but he'd spent enough on the gear that a couple hundred dollars more on astronomy programs seemed like a step too far. If all of his math had been right, he would have a time lapse of the moon's entire trip from horizon to horizon, with the moment of total lunar eclipse framed perfectly between the branches of the tree.

He ran the whole motion through at max speed. As far as he could tell, it was going to work. Now all there was to do was reset, start the official timer, and cross his fingers.

A few hours later, Alan sat cross-legged in his tent, watching the camera do its thing. The tracking was going flawlessly, and every thirty seconds or so he was treated to the click of a shutter. The moon had been out for a while, and the camera had kept its eye on the prize. Just a few minutes ago, a little bite had appeared out of the corner of the moon, signaling the start of the lunar eclipse. It would take about three hours to run its course, but he didn't have anything better to do than sip from his thermos of tomato soup and indulge in a rare moment of calm and serenity.

His old nemesis, the mobile phone, once again had other plans. This particular ringtone was a grating pop song he hated. Normally, he wouldn't have chosen it, but it just so happened it perfectly set the mood for the calls that came in from that number.

"Hello, Fontaine Freelance, Alan speaking. How may I help you today?" he said, expertly masking his irritation with professional courtesy.

"Fontaine. Cox here."

"Good evening, Mr. Cox," he said. "Let me just say that I am honored that you would take time out of your busy evening to call me so late at—"

"Can it, Fontaine. They added some more dates to the festival. I'm going to need you."

"What day did you have in mind?"

"Friday. All day. Saturday and Sunday, too."

"This Friday, sir?"

"No. Next year. Of course this Friday. It's festival season."

"But that's the day after tomorrow. I guess there must have been some scheduling snafu, but I was supposed to be off the freelance calendar for this whole week. I had a sabbatical planned, followed by—"

"I don't give a crap what you had planned. I need every camera on hand. You know how much of a pain it is running this site out of Philadelphia? We are going to make damn sure this film festival is the biggest thing on the East Coast, so it comes back bigger and better next year, and I can keep the gold mine running on the regular. That means saturation, Fontaine. Full saturation. TV, print, Web. I want nothing but photos of the New Philly Film Fest, and I want nothing but my watermark on all of them. So you get here bright and early Friday, you take the assignment I give you, or I'm pulling your name from the rotation."

Alan gritted his teeth. He hoped it wasn't audible over the phone. "Yes, sir. Thank you, sir."

Cox grunted, as close as he typically got to an actual sign-off, and hung up. Alan took a slow breath.

"Could've been worse, Alan. It could have been tonight." He let a shudder of irritation flutter over him. "Wouldn't have been the first time."

He thumbed his way through his text threads until he found "Jessie (Police)."

Hey, Jessie. Sorry for the short notice, but I'm going to have to bow out on the meeting we set up on Saturday. Freelance work.

Almost immediately, his phone rang. It was her.

"Hello?" he said.

"Are you standing me up, Alan?" said the voice on the other line.

"I didn't mean to bother you so late at night."

"Are you standing me up, Alan?" she said again, some playful force behind the question, but with a bit more intensity this time.

"It's the festival. Cox wants me on hand for the whole thing."

"Alan, there's this amazing new word you should learn. I believe it's pronounced 'no.' I hear it works wonders."

"I'm not in a business where I can afford to be turning down work. Do you know how many people actually pay their bills with photography? We're like unicorns."

"Yeah, yeah. I know. We've had this conversation before, which is why I find it kind of nuts that you'd pass up a chance to interview for the force. It is *rare* for a precinct this size to hire from the outside for a forensic photographer."

"If I turn Cox down and he blacklists me, I'm done for."

"If you get this job, you won't *need* him."

"Mom always said you should take the sure thing over the long shot."

"*My* mom always said you miss one hundred percent of the shots you don't take."

"I didn't know your mom was Wayne Gretzky."

"Look, I'm not going to tell you what to do. Hell, if I *did* tell you what to do, your head would probably explode like a malfunctioning robot when you realized you couldn't people-please two people at once. But if you skip this one, I'm not so sure you'll get another shot."

"I know, but..."

"I know I know. Take the sure thing. Are you at least going to be able to take those pictures you wanted to take?"

"I'm already working on it. The time lapse is going."

"Wait, the eclipse is going? It's overcast here."

"Crystal clear up here. I'll have to send you the time lapse when it's done."

"You better. Anyway, I'll see you when I see you."

"Same. So long."

She hung up and he shook his head again. It felt bad to say no. It *always* felt bad to say no, but it was doubly so for Jessie. No one in Alan's life had done him more favors than she had, and vice versa. He didn't even want to think about how many strings she'd had to pull to get him the interview. But money was money. He had to pay his bills.

Alan plugged his phone into a portable power brick and yawned. He hadn't done much more than drive for most of the day, but he was exhausted. When he got overtired, it caused him all sorts of problems. His hands got shaky—a real problem for a photographer. He couldn't sit still. It was like he'd never shaken the "get cranky and fussy when you're overtired" reflex from infancy. Considering there was a long way to go before the time-lapse experiment was done, and he'd prefer to be sharp for the crucial bit in the middle, he decided it was best to take a nap now. He set an alarm for five minutes before totality, zipped up the tent flap, and slid into his sleeping bag for a snooze.

He blinked his eyes and glanced around, disoriented. Things around him looked familiar, but he couldn't shake the feeling that they *shouldn't*. This wasn't a place he should have ever returned to, but here he was. A worn desktop lay before him, its veneer carved by the surgically sharp point of a grade-school compass of a dozen generations of students. The walls were covered with vaguely educational posters providing lessons in simple math and grammar. Rows of desks ran along either side of him, populated by faces he couldn't quite place.

This was school, he knew that much. But it didn't seem right. It felt like it was a seventh-grade classroom at the most. But the people sitting around him in their little individual desks felt more like high school or college types. His dream-addled mind grappled with the faulty logic in the way most sleeping brains did—by completely embracing it as the unquestioned reality of the moment.

"… Now, as you all know, I consider the take-home assignments to be of equal, if not greater, importance to anything you might be graded upon in class," the teacher announced from the front of the room.

His heart dropped at the sound of the voice. Not him. Not *him*. It was Dr. Pendergrass. It was fair to say that most students had moments when they thought the teacher had a grudge against them, but Alan was absolutely convinced that Dr. Pendergrass's one goal in life was to fail him. He never bothered trying to figure out why. For someone as easily cowed by authority as Alan, teachers were like forces of nature. He wouldn't ask why the storm chose to strike him with lightning, and he wouldn't ask why Dr. Pendergrass always managed to find a way to call on him for the hardest question in a given assignment. Luckily, there hadn't been any homework the night before.

"I want you all to take out last night's assignment," Dr. Pendergrass said.

A bolt of burning anxiety ripped through him. All around him, the other students were dutifully slipping composition pads from their bags and flipping them open. He numbly pulled his drawstring backpack to his lap to try to find his own book. The pack felt far too light to contain the texts for this class. As he tried to open the bag, he found his fingers were too clumsy to undo the slipknot.

"No, no, no," he muttered, watching the wave of students answering their questions work its way up and down the rows beside him.

The more anxious he got, the more he fumbled with the slipknot. Why couldn't he get his hands to work?

Mounting frustration mixed with the sting of the inevitable discovery that he'd not done his homework was a potent and debilitating cocktail. Gradually, though, he found that there was something else going on around him.

He took his attention off the bag and looked around. The walls seemed... wrong. Even more wrong than they had been a moment ago. They were wavering, hazy. Less real than they were before. And it was darker than it should have been. Not like the sun had been setting or the lights had been dimmed, but like darkness had somehow seeped through the walls like a fog. It felt cold. His skin tingled. His brain felt itchy, like little prickly claws were poking and tugging at it. If he could have crawled out of his own skin to get away from the terrible bone-deep unease, he would have.

A long shadow spread across the room, seeming to cast itself *through* the wall. He had a hard time making out the details as it projected across the students' desks, but it seemed to have a forked, split shape. Something distant in his mind recognized it as the tree he'd hiked to find. He turned to the source of the shadow and was treated to a fleeting glimpse of the tree itself, but like the rest of the room, it was wrong. What he knew to be a craggy gray trunk against a starry black sky was quite the opposite.

The sky was almost painful to look upon, a photo-negative of the night he remembered.

He shook. Icy fingers felt like they were tightening around his heart. A horrid sensation spread through him, a scoring, tearing feeling that left him feeling hollowed out. Alan shivered and gripped his bag tight until the feeling faded. It didn't vanish. If it was the chill of a cold winter night, what he felt now was the warmth of a blanket thrown over him. It wasn't enough to erase what he'd felt, but it reminded him of what it felt like before...

"Alan?" came the teacher's voice.

The classroom snapped instantly back to normal, and though the residue of the sensation lingered, he turned to the teacher like a deer caught in headlights.

"Uh, yeah? Yes! Yes, Mr. Pendergrass. *Doctor!* Dr. Pendergrass," he said.

"Perhaps you'd like to answer the question?"

He fought his bag open and pulled out the notebook. "I... uh..." He cleared his throat. "Could you repeat the question?"

"It is question six from the homework assignment."

His chest felt like there was a lump of hot lead sitting on it. Tears were forming in his eyes. Page after page of his notebook was completely blank.

"I don't... uh... I didn't..."

"You *are* aware that this assignment is worth twenty percent of your grade," the professor rumbled.

"I must have... I don't remember you assigning it..."

He flinched as a piece of paper executed an odd, unnatural loop into his vision and flopped onto the desk in front of him. He stared in confusion at the slip of paper, which didn't look like the white page with blue lines that had defined the bulk of his educational career. It felt rough. The color was oddly textured, like it had been shaded with a charcoal pencil.

The teacher's impatience boiled as he flipped open the page. A curious bit of penmanship traced out an even more curious message.

"Mr. Fontaine?" the teacher said impatiently. "Either answer the question, or you get a zero for the assignment!"

"Th-the answer is. Uh... Two sprigs of onyx leaf combined with twice-boiled brine of the ashen sea, simmered with the bones of three hearty joints of beast for a night and a day."

He looked to the teacher, fully prepared for a gale-force scolding. Perhaps there would be a peppering of chortles from the rest of the class.

"That is correct," the teacher said. His disappointment at missing the chance to reprimand Alan was palpable.

Alan cocked his head and looked around, anticipating some sort of prank. "That's correct?"

"Yes, Mr. Fontaine."

"But this is Linear Algebra class."

"And you have answered the question properly."

The teacher moved on, leaving Alan to slump into his seat and enjoy the most magnificent wave of relief in recent memory as it swept over him. After a few moments, though, he found himself considering the paper. He knew he hadn't written the message. Someone had passed it to him. He turned and looked for a likely candidate. One person instantly stood out from the rest.

She was distinctive looking, to put it lightly. Her skin was pale, and her features oddly defined. The lines of her face shuddered and moved about like the sketch lines of a quickly cobbled-together animation. Her hair was long and black and fluttered in a breeze that didn't seem to affect anyone or anything around her. She had a satisfied grin on her face and a pile of the same rough pages on her desk.

"Excuse me. Were you the one who gave me the answer?" he whispered to her.

The woman's large eyes darted up to meet his, and for a moment she looked as petrified as he'd been under the teacher's gaze.

"What? No! Why would you think that?"

He pointed. "You've got a stack of the fancy paper there. And a fancy pen."

She glanced back and forth between her desk and his finger. "No I don't!" She swept her hand across her desk. The pages fluttered up into the air, and then they were gone. They spread like smoke or blown dust and simply dissipated.

Alan blinked and waved off the fumes, but like so many other inexplicable things in the last few minutes, the oddness rolled off him. "Well, thanks for the help." He held out his hand to her for a shake. "I'm Alan. And you are?"

His mysterious helper leaned away from his hand as though it was threatening to bite her.

"Wake up! Now!"

Alan snorted and opened his eyes. As one does after a strange dream, he took a few moments to acclimate to the real world again, then slowly slid upright and wiped the sleep from his eyes.

"Oof. That was a weird one," he said, the scattered images of his unusual dream sliding into the shadows of his mind.

Thirty seconds or so of staring blankly finally instilled the motivation and insight to realize that something was amiss. He glanced at his phone, which had a notification that he'd missed an alarm. While helpful, that wasn't terribly necessary, because he already had a far better indicator that he'd overslept in that the sun was already up, shining through the thin nylon of his tent.

"Don't be screwed up, don't be screwed up," he muttered as he hastily unzipped the tent.

The camera had been out in the cold all night, which he would normally not tolerate. Precipitation, frost, strong wind, any number of things could foul the sensitive bits of apparatus that were responsible for one hundred percent of his income. He gave it a cursory glance and found it to be in one piece, with no obvious damage. The monster of a battery he had attached to it even still had some charge in it. He clicked it off the sophisticated pan-and-tilt rig and flipped through the pictures. There were hundreds of them, as there should have been, and the moon was nicely centered in every single one. As far as he could tell, he got the full time lapse along with enough shots of the camera's final position to fill up the memory card. He lingered in the total-eclipse portion of the shot, gazing at the camera's screen. That was the most critical bit, and the bit he was most concerned about. The exposure settings he'd programmed in were best guesses, but if he didn't get close enough, he might not be able to tweak it enough to make it look and feel the way he'd intended. Aside from some oddly pronounced motes of shadowy contrast around the tree, it looked like he had a winner, or at least the ingredients for one.

"No harm done," he said with a huff of relief.

As quickly as he had assembled all of his equipment, it took twice as long for him to disassemble it since he took care to investigate each and every bit of his gear to see if accidentally getting a full night's sleep had any consequences. One of the batteries looked like it might have gotten wet, but not enough to overcome the vaguely defined "weather resistant" nature of the device.

Bit by bit, the equipment, then the tent found their way to their proper places, and he was ready to be on his way. With his pack on his back, he took a few steps toward the car, but a thought occurred to him. This was it. This was the last time he was likely to see this place. He tried not to be too sentimental, but a big piece of his childhood had been spent here.

Alan trudged up to the tree and placed his hand on the surface. It had always been a bit of an oddball. Dead for as long as he could remember but never taken down by the elements. A lone tree on the top of a hill that he couldn't imagine would have been planted by the farmer who used to own this place. Nothing about it quite made sense. Maybe that was why he and his siblings were so fascinated by it. That, or because it was easy to climb. He grabbed hold of one of the two main branches and tested it. Still plenty sturdy, it seemed. He pulled himself up a bit to find where he'd carved his name. He smiled, then glanced aside to find some fresh marks in the tree. They were claw marks, deep gouges in the tree that couldn't be more than a few weeks old, from the way the wood at the base wasn't faded by the sun yet. He grabbed his phone and snapped a picture—blasphemy for a photographer to use a phone, but the good camera was already packed up. He then took a few more shots of the tree and the various carvings by him and his cousins before giving it another thoughtful pat.

"So long, buddy," he said. "With any luck, that eclipse and this camera will give you some new life. And maybe it'll help make a dent in mine."

Chapter 2

B y the time Alan was navigating the thickening traffic on the outskirts of Philadelphia, the sun was down again. Between oversleeping and his admittedly conservative driving habits, the entire day had been spent either on the road or at rest stops. That was enough time for him to get sick of the selection of music he'd loaded on his phone. Rather than endure the current state of pop music or burn some data on his mobile, he decided to switch to a news station to see if the world had managed to become any more of a trash fire than it had been when he left for his little trip.

Astoundingly, it had.

"... an alarming uptick in home invasions in the New York-Canada border over the course of the last eight hours," dictated a calm-voiced newsreader. "Some of the smaller cities in the region of the crime wave have reported fewer than ten break-ins in the last year, but have suffered as many as fifty in just the last few hours."

Alan whistled. "I guess that chain on the land might have been a good idea after all."

"The police chief of Plattsburg, New York, was interviewed on the crisis and had this to say." A harsher, less radio-worthy voice replaced the newsreader, half-buried in the murmur of reporters at whatever passed for a press conference in Upstate New York. "I want everyone to know that law enforcement is doing everything that can be done, but there is no reason to believe that this is anything other than an isolated incident. There was a rush of tourists to the area thanks to the eclipse. This was probably the work of out-of-towners. And I... ahem... let's make this clear. I'm not saying the eclipse had anything to do with it. Just the tourists who came to see it and chose to disrespect the locals and their property."

The newsreader cut back in, but Alan turned off the radio.

"Some people just shouldn't be trusted to do public speaking."

He reached for his cupholder to where he'd stowed his thermal mug of coffee, but when he lifted it, there was barely a slosh.

"Did I finish that already?" he muttered. "Man. And I can barely keep my eyes open. I've got to start taking it easy. I wonder of you can build up a tolerance for coffee. If this keeps up, I'm going to have to switch to those energy shots."

He turned down the block containing his apartment building and rolled down his window to swipe his pass for the parking structure. Already he was starting to work through what it would take to meet his obligations for the next day.

"Get the stuff up to the room, back up the photos, see how the time lapse came out. Maybe some TV? Dinner. Gotta do dinner. I hope I have one of those freezer dinners left. I'd hate to have to wait for delivery, let alone pay for it. Alarm, bright and early. Head to Cox's place, see what he's got for me."

He rubbed his eyes. "Maybe I'll be done in time for the police interview? Ha... Fat chance of that."

Though his glorified gossip magnate of a boss did his best to avoid showing it, there was little doubt that he knew an eye for photography when he saw it. The man knew Alan's pictures were some of the best his firm had in their archives, and he'd do what it took to make sure Alan couldn't or wouldn't find work elsewhere. A man more confident in his chances elsewhere would have quit long ago, but for the last eighteen months Alan had covered the vast majority of his living expenses from Cox's assignments. He could float for *maybe* two weeks on credit if he lost this job, and two weeks wasn't a lot of time to find a new photography gig that paid nearly as much. For now, he'd have to deal with the short leash Cox kept him on.

"Not again..." he grumbled as he reached the top level of the parking deck.

Parking spots were assigned for residents in his building, and they were laid out roughly the same way the apartments were. That meant that you parked next to your neighbors. On his right, his neighbor Mr. Brooks was parked just fine, as he always was. The man was in his late eighties, and it was entirely possible he'd not moved his car since 2006. The car to the left belonged to Ms. Levitt.

"There is no way this is not on purpose," he grumbled.

His neighbor's car, an SUV that was already a bit of a tight fit for a standard parking space, was parked at a downright drunken angle. No credence was paid to the lines between the spots, and the bumper was positioned with mathematical precision to be as close as humanly possible to blocking Alan's spot without *actually* blocking his spot. He spent fifteen minutes lining up his car to thread the needle. Side mirrors folded in, window rolled down so he could eyeball the gap. When he finally parked, he didn't even bother seeing if he could open his door enough to get out. Instead, he did what had become an all-too-familiar maneuver. He climbed over the seats and made his way out the back hatch, nearly spilling his camping and camera supplies onto the ground as he did.

When the entire frustrating endeavor was handled, he dusted himself off and started gathering his stuff.

"Home sweet home..."

His more ambitious plans for the evening quickly slid from his brain once he dropped off the last of his bags. The couch was calling his name, and a belly that had received only black coffee and truck-stop food demanded something a bit more nutritious, or at least more filling.

Alan's apartment was meager, but that suited him fine. He was always more about working than leisure time. He had a den with a nice big TV that he typically ignored in favor of his laptop screen. He shuffled into a kitchen barely large enough to feed a bachelor and its associated "dining room" that would be lucky to seat two people. He opened the freezer to discover the only thing inside was a single store-brand microwave dinner.

"'Salisbury Steak,'" he observed, wiping the frost from the top of the box. "A food that exists only in cafeterias and freezer cases."

He slapped the food in the microwave and washed his hands and face in his tiny bathroom.

Something caught his eye and he turned. There was nothing but his shadow, though he could swear even as he watched it, it shuddered and twitched. He glanced up and flicked the light bulb.

"I'll replace that next week. Probably time to go LED on it anyway..."

Alan fetched his food from the microwave and turned on some mindless television. The other plans for the evening evaporated as he let himself slip into a near-vegetative state. His mind ran in pointless little circles. Alan's opinion of modern television was a near match for his opinion of modern music, but TV served its purpose of rounding over the sharp corners of a long, unproductive day and easing him toward something resembling relaxation.

Slowly, blissfully, the world started to slide away. He could feel the puffy clouds of a light doze start to claim him, and the forms that rose up out of the fog were some of his favorites. College. Probably the happiest time of his life. Already he could see the walls of his dorm room, not so much smaller than his little apartment. He started to lose himself in what he hoped would be a rare, happy recurring dream about the time he'd—

SLAM *SLAM* *SLAM*

He jerked to wakefulness again with a jolt of panic at the sudden noise. A few moments of mental floundering anchored him in reality again. He snapped on the light and tried to blink the heaviness from his eyes.

"I know you're in there, Mr. Fontaine," called an angry woman from the other side of the door.

"I'm coming, Ms. Levitt," he called back, teetering with not-yet-fully restored equilibrium to his hallway door.

Alan's life had been shaped primarily by angry authority figures who rattled his nerves. He had no shortage of them at work and school. Ms.

Levitt was the one fate had assigned to his personal life. And she was an overachiever. The parking stunts were the least of her contributions to his general misery.

He opened the door and squinted at the bright light of the hallway.

Ms. Levitt was a woman in her thirties who had earned the adjective "crotchety" about three decades too early. From the way she hectored and bullied those around her, you'd think she should have been the head mistress of an Edwardian boarding school for orphaned girls, not a middle-aged dance instructor. She shoved an envelope in his face.

"Another letter. Your name. My address," she growled.

"I'm sorry, Ms. Levitt."

"Don't be sorry, *fix it!*"

He read the envelope, but there was really no need. This wasn't a new problem. It would be the museum's accounting department. It always was.

"It's from my old job. They have the address wrong. I've tried to—"

"I don't want to hear excuses, Mr. Fontaine. I've already informed building management."

"No... Ms. Levitt, if I get enough strikes, they're going to take my building discount on the parking spot."

"You should have thought of that before you started cluttering my mailbox with *your* mail. And keep your TV down. I can hear it through the vent, and it is *very* inconsiderate."

"I'm sorry, Ms. Levitt."

She gave him the sort of look usually reserved for vermin eating out of her trash and stomped back to her own apartment. He shut his door and tossed the envelope on a side table with the last three he'd received.

"That'll be another forty dollars a month. Just what I need."

Rather than fritter away any more of the night dozing on the couch with reality TV numbing his senses, he decided to turn in. He hung his pants on a chair to be worn another day—a habit that Jessie had dubbed "dorm laundry"—and slid under the covers.

As Murphy's Law would have it, while he had barely been able to keep his eyes open while driving home and watching TV, the moment his head hit the pillow his mind latched on to all of the concerns and annoyances of the day and put them on an endless loop. His half-lidded eyes stared hazily at the walls of the bedroom. This was the one part of the house he'd actually taken the time to make his own. A small desk in the corner served as his office, and the walls served as his gallery.

Some of the best photos of his career were framed, covering the wall in a haphazard collage. It was a curated collection. He liked to kid himself that this was the assortment he would display if he were ever invited to do an art show. Not the group gallery that had failed to make him any money a few days ago; but a real show built around him. He would call it "Shades of Shadow." His theme, which had emerged quite by accident, was the contrast of light and shadow. For as long as he could remember, he'd been drawn to it. One of his earliest memories was his grandfather showing him how to make shadow puppets with an old camping lantern against the wall of his tent. He'd thought it was pure magic at the time.

Cars passing below cast soft, shifting shadows on the walls. They seemed to move with purpose, lingering here and there. He grinned faintly as sleep finally started to take him. Maybe one day, if he had a real gallery, there'd be a person casting that shadow, considering a photo of another person casting another shadow. And so on, and so on, and so on...

"Come on, come on!" he shouted, hauling a heavy wheeled camera case.

It staggered and shuddered as he pulled it, lurching to and fro like a disobedient shopping cart. Ahead of him, the crew door to a huge stadium loomed. This was a big-ticket job: a concert or something similar. He had to do behind-the-scenes shots for a documentary. According to the ticket, stage time was 9:15 p.m. According to his watch, it was 9:12 p.m.

"Why is this thing so busted?" he growled, tugging at the case.

A frustrated tug hauled it off balance, and it fell over. The latches gave out, and it practically exploded into a scattering of lenses, gels, batteries, and harnesses.

"No!" he cried, gathering as much of the equipment as he could and stuffing it back inside.

He clicked the case shut and abandoned rolling it entirely. Instead, he heaved it from the ground and ran toward the crew door. Barely three strides away, a promoter stepped into the doorway and slammed it shut.

"Wait!" he called, hammering on the door. "You've got to let me in. I can't miss the shot of them taking the stage. It's the whole reason I'm here!"

After two more fruitless thumps on the door, he turned and leaned against the wall beside it.

"That's it..." he muttered. "That's it. No one will ever hire a camera guy again if he can't be trusted to be backstage in time for the curtain." He gritted his teeth. "Why did I think I could do this? You're worthless, Alan." He pushed away from the wall and grappled with his case. "That's it. I'm done. Enough of this stupid thing. I've wasted enough time trying to..."

He trailed off as he heard a faint click from the door. When he turned, he saw it was slowly swinging open. Alan's heart leaped into his throat, and he frantically hefted the case and hurried to catch the door.

It swung open easily with a light nudge, and he rushed through. Directly ahead, he could see the band still preparing. He hadn't missed his chance! He hurried forward a few steps, ready to catch the precious moment that could save his career. But then he stopped. The door hadn't just opened itself. Someone had done him a solid, letting him in.

He turned. A dark form vanished into the dimly lit side hall leading back into the labyrinth of equipment behind the stage. Something about the way the person moved, the way the person *felt*, was jarring in a very real way. It was like he'd been on autopilot, and with the appearance of that half-seen figure, he'd been shaken back to his senses.

"Wait... Since when was I supposed to be doing a concert?" he said, logic seeping in.

Alan turned back to the stage and the band. They looked just the same as they had before, but at the same time they didn't seem real to him anymore. It wasn't like he was looking at a real band. He was looking at what he imagined a real band might look like. This was a dream.

And yet, the click and thump of his unseen benefactor's hurrying footsteps lacked the same ethereal sense. They were very much real, or at least more real than anything else around him. He dropped his case and rushed off after the footsteps. If this was a dream, he could at least focus on the most intriguing part of it.

The backstage area stretched on ahead of him, farther than any real stage should. And as he twisted and turned his way deeper among the towering speaker cabinets and scaffolds, things started to change. It was like his mind was running out of concert-type-things and was steadily drawing other set pieces from other dreams. One turn sent him down a hallway in the hospital where his mother worked. Another brought him to the frozen-food aisle of his local supermarket. He could feel that he was gaining on the figure running from him.

By the time he could see the figure with enough clarity to know that it was a woman, the setting around him had gone past the familiar and into the bizarre. The walls were rough and desaturated. Everything was either jet black or harsh white. He couldn't make out the details of the ground, but each pounding step sank into it with a dusty crunch, like he was wading through the remnants of an old campfire.

Alan reached out and caught the shoulder of the woman running from him. He spun her around.

Large, anxious eyes stared into his. Her face was instantly recognizable. It was the same sketchy, shifting face of the woman from the previous night's dream. Normally, he could barely remember the broad strokes of a dream, but this face felt burned into his mind, and here it was again.

He looked her up and down. She was shorter than he was, her long hair roiling around her head like boiling ink. Her pupils were elongated, almost catlike, but with a more complex, faceted shape. The features clashed and flickered over more human versions of the same anatomy.

"Who are you?" he said.

She pressed herself against the wall. Somehow the hallway had closed itself off into a dead end. When she spoke, it was with a thin veneer of command and authority stretched over a bottomless well of fear.

"I'm no one. Just ignore me. I'm trying to make things better for both of us, that's all. Just wake up, or you'll be late again!" She pointed a small, cunning finger at him. "And don't forget the coffee!"

Alan's eyes snapped open. Sunlight poured into his room, casting his shadow starkly on the wall. He squinted against the bright light and stumbled out of bed to shut the shade. Gradually, his brain flipped on the various senses. Eventually, he realized that an odd, annoying twitch he felt every few moments was actually his alarm.

He looked to the clock: 7:19. It'd been going off for four minutes. He slapped the button to silence the alarm and clawed his fingers through his hair. He'd slept straight through the night. He couldn't remember the last time he'd done that, and now he'd done it twice in a row. Normally, he'd toss and turn endlessly. Sleeping the sleep of the dead evidently didn't do the body as much good as he'd hoped it would, as he was still utterly exhausted. He briefly considered sleeping in, but his sputtering brain was able to dredge up the fact that his vacation/sabbatical had been cut short and he was due at the assignment meeting at Cox Media in a little over an hour. Which meant he actually only had about a half hour, since it was largely first come, first serve, and the good assignments went quick.

The quickest shower he could manage while still convincing himself he'd done his hygienic duty was followed by his patented "brush in the apartment, floss in the drive-through" technique. Yes, it meant he brushed *before* he ate, but it saved him five precious minutes.

He tugged on yesterday's pants and today's shirt and hit the road. His frugal side winced at the fact that breakfast would have to come from a coffee shop. At least if he was going to waste money in the interest of time, he could convince himself he was helping a local business, though. His favorite coffee shop was a rare reversal. It was a mom-and-pop shop that had moved into the carcass of a Starbucks that had closed. They'd semicleverly renamed the place Vice Versa and had had the good sense to keep the drive-through in operation.

"Morning, Alex," said the woman at the window.

"Alan."

"Right, right. What'll it be?"

"A cheese Danish. And a medium—" *Large.* "Large coffee." He shook his head. That was odd.

The woman at the window laughed. "Which is it, medium or large?"

Large. "Large please. Black. With three stirrers."

"Coming right up."

She paced off to fill his order, leaving him to grapple with just what exactly his brain was up to. He'd had his clashes with impulse control. Everyone did. But his notions had never been quite so vocal. The word thumped into his mind like someone had written a note and lobbed it at him in Algebra class.

Since this was very likely a symptom of his still-awakening mind, and thus would soon be solved by the forthcoming coffee, he decided to turn on the radio to distract himself from his own confusion.

"... last minute touchdown gave another win to the Eagles. Final score, 27 to 16. In other news, incumbent Senator Savage has taken a commanding lead in the polls with just weeks to go before the midterms. In hopes of solidifying his base, he has agreed to attend a charity dinner and art auction being thrown as part of the New Philly Film Fest."

Alan whistled. "That's going to be a photographic gold mine," he murmured. "Beloved politician at a charity event while the town's awash in film stars. No wonder Cox wanted all hands on deck."

"We've got a black coffee and a Danish for Alex!" the woman said, marching back up to the window.

"Alan, actually," he corrected again.

"Right. Sorry. Alan. That'll be six dollars."

His internal accountant slapped him in the back of the head and reminded him that the same breakfast would have cost him less than a dollar at home. He took the bag of morning essentials and dug into his pocket for the money.

"What the..."

Beside his wallet was a handful of bills. He never kept bills separate from his wallet. When he pulled them free, he found that it was a badly crumpled trio of weirdly dusty twenties.

"Oh man, jackpot," he said.

Suddenly not feeling quite so bad about breakfast, Alan tossed the coffee clerk one of the twenties and peeled off a couple of bucks from the change as a tip. Typically, he would have lingered long enough to finagle the food and drink into something a little more amenable to vehicular consumption, but it was suddenly far more important than he'd realized to get to this assignment meeting. If he got some good shots of celebrities rubbing elbows with politicians, he could probably make enough on the pictures to cover the rest of his month's expenses in a single night. He pulled out and drove away. Wrestling the coffee into the cupholder and shoving the Danish into his mouth would have to wait for the first red light. He made his way toward the day job just as quickly as his Goody-Two-shoes-level adherence to traffic laws would allow.

A few minutes later, Alan was hustling into the main meeting room of Cox Media. About a dozen other people with varying claims to the job title of journalist were there waiting. These ranged from frazzle-haired college students looking for some extra cash to suspenders-wearing old-schoolers looking to supplement their pensions. Every time he wandered into this place, he wondered how exactly it could still be in operation. In a world of websites and the gig economy, the idea of requiring his employees to assemble at an actual physical location to get their assignments for the day was charmingly anachronistic. But, then, that was Mr. Cox in a nutshell. The specifics of the man's history were the subject of many rumors and few facts, but the broad strokes seemed to be that he came from old money and had enough of a bankroll to endure at least a few more years of this painfully inefficient little enterprise before he'd have to pull the rip cord on his golden parachute.

As if summoned by his musing, Cox himself marched into the conference room. His face was perpetually beet red, as though just moments before appearing he'd been sprinting up a flight of stairs. The man had a double chin and a roll of fat above the collar on the back of his head that Alan chose to dub his third chin. This was a rather distinctive feature, as he was otherwise rather fit. It gave him the look of a man who'd cinched his bow tie too tight and was slowly inflating his own head. Combined with the fiery-orange hair, this had earned him the nickname of Red, though very few employees actually called him that, for reasons that were obvious in a school-boy-snicker sort of way.

He clapped his hands as he marched in, flanked as always by his assistant, who looked like a younger, more harried version of himself. Folks called him Little Red, though mostly behind his back. Other times he was just Jerry.

"Okay, okay, okay, sports fans," Cox said. "For the next week, we are going to be flooding the streets. For once, no trips to Manhattan or Atlantic City or Washington DC, or any of that are necessary. Hollywood is shipping their brightest stars right here to the city of brotherly love."

"It's mostly indies," remarked a short, slightly portly woman near the front of the gathered photo pool.

She was Marie-Anna Proctor. If this had been a classroom, she would have been the teacher's pet. Since it *wasn't* a classroom, the popular consensus was that she was Mr. Cox's mistress. Whatever the nature of their relationship, the woman could do no wrong, getting away with a snideness that would get half of the other photographers kicked out of the meeting.

"Right, right. Indies. Even better. They're just like regular celebrities, but without the stink of old Hollywood on them. Hipsters eat that up."

"Millennials," Marie-Anna said.

"What?"

"They're called 'millennials' now."

"Fine, whatever. I have copy writers for that. The point is, we can stay local and not get stuck with local talent. Now that means a lot of stuff, not the least of which is you're going to be out there competing with the big boys, just like you would be if we'd shipped you out and about. But they don't have what we have, which is a knowledge, inside and out, of every last morsel of this city. So we can find the best spots, and faster. Everyone got that? I expect you to outmaneuver those out-of-town chumps. So line up! Let's get these assignments handed out."

Everyone filed together and got in line. Marie-Anna, in complete contradiction to schoolyard protocol, cut the line entirely. No one minded, or at least no one expected any different.

Mr. Cox pulled a stack of handwritten index cards from his pocket and started riffling through them. He peeled off three of them and handed them to Marie-Anna.

"You know the drill. See Jerry about the extras and such," he said.

"Sure thing, sugar," she said, grinning at him with a sweetness completely absent elsewhere in her demeanor.

One by one, the rest of the pool stepped forward.

Alan managed to get to the middle of the line without cutting or shoving. Other freelancers poured in as the assignments continued, those who were more interested in avoiding Cox's pep talks than getting the choice assignments. They would end up getting the crumbs at the bottom of the bag, though being near the front of the line was never a sure route to a juicy assignment either. As each photographer stepped up, Cox flipped through his deck of cards and selected a few. Ostensibly, this was to assign jobs to people according to their strengths. It wouldn't have surprised Alan if he was picking them at random.

When Alan got to the front, Mr. Cox spread the deck and leafed through.

"There you go. Airport. Jerry will give you the bounty list for photos and the arrivals list for the day," he said.

"The airport," Alan said, looking over the card. "You called me in from a sabbatical to go to the airport to get arrival shots?"

"We need every picture we can get."

Grab all the cards.

Alan's hand twitched as he found himself nearly acting on the impulse. "Maybe you could give me a backup job, just in case the other people you've assigned to the airport end up having it under control?"

"Maybe I could take the airport cards back and send you home empty-handed. Card assignments are final. The cards are law," Cox said. "Now head out. The first arrivals are probably already on their way in for a landing."

Grab all the cards.

Alan pushed the impulse aside and took the arrivals printout from Jerry. With his assignment in hand, he paced off toward the exit. Marie-Anna leaned against the doorway, her stack of cards in one hand and her phone in the other. She was busy tapping in the information to build her agenda for the night, but she needn't have bothered. If this was anything like any other assignment meeting, she'd be heading to one of three hot spots around town. Good lighting, expensive drinks, and as a result, good pictures of rich people. The fact that a laminated badge was sticking out of her bag suggested she'd also gotten backstage credentials for something or another. She always got the cherry on the top of the sundae.

Steal all her cards.

He shut his eyes for a moment. When he opened them again, Marie-Anna was glancing at him wearily.

"Can I help you, Adam?"

"Alan. And no, I'm sorry. Just a little distracted today. Good luck with the assignment."

"Mm-hmm. You too," she said without a drop of sincerity or interest.

Alan continued out the door and hurried down the hall. "The devil on my shoulder is *awfully* loud these days."

A few hours later, Alan was huddled in his parka, standing outside and watching the sky. There were all sorts of rules about where you could take pictures at an airport, and of whom. Most of those rules were unwritten and depended almost entirely on the whims of airport staff. One of the more unseemly things he'd had to learn was how to circumvent them. It involved a lot of standing outside, but there were a handful of places where he could park himself and still be able to hear announcements and squint at a distant arrivals board. A cool day was heading into a bitter night now, and he'd only crossed off half the names on his photo list. The weather forecast called for a snowstorm. In Upstate New York, that would be no big deal. But here in Philly, it was throwing the whole city into a tizzy. Flights were delayed or canceled. He sipped his coffee, the third of the night, and heaved a sigh.

"I think we've seen as many as we're going to see," he said to himself.

He paced toward the parking structure and flicked through the images he'd taken. Among Cox's more bizarre requirements was the one to double submit everything. Not only did he require a reasonably immediate digital delivery of the photos that might be worth printing, but he also required the memory card itself. It was all part of an exclusivity agreement that he either didn't realize or didn't care was utterly pointless and trivial to circumvent. Most of the other photographers made copies of their memory cards before handing them over. Heck, most of them took the stipend he gave to buy replacements, then bought cheaper ones off eBay and pocketed the difference. Chances were pretty good Alan himself was the only one who followed the policy to the letter.

On his way into the parking structure, he drained the rest of his coffee and tossed it in the nearest trash can.

"Pardon me. Sir?"

Alan turned. A pair of men trotted toward him. They looked rather unassuming, though certainly not normal. Each man wore a sincere attempt at the same outfit. The near-uniform included a coat, longer than a jacket but shorter than a trench. Each was some shade on the darker end of the blue spectrum. They were fastened with polished silver buttons. One man anxiously jangled a key chain from his gloved hand. The other had his hands in his pockets. The whole thing screamed "well-meaning religious recruitment." He'd always heard they were a staple of airports, but until now he'd really not had to deal with them.

"Can I have a word with you?" said the key-chain dangler.

"Um, sure," he said unenthusiastically.

There were few things he wanted to do *less* than learn about their particular brand of salvation, but there was such a thing as courtesy.

"You look like you were hanging around for quite a while today," the first man said, fiddling with his key chain and glancing at it periodically.

"Yeah. It's part of the job. There's a festival in town, and my boss wanted some shots of the arriving celebrities."

"Did you see anyone good?" said the shorter of the pair, eyebrows raised in genuine interest.

"Well, a lot of the flights were canceled, and the really big celebrities are starting to get wily. But I got a few."

"Can I see?" he said, edging closer and trying to peer over the camera hanging at Alan's neck.

"Uh, no. I mean, yes, you'll probably see them, but you'll have to check out the usual star gossip sites and such."

"Oh, come on. You can show me."

He shook his head. "Part of the contract. Cox Media gets first look and first distribution rights."

Run.

Alan shook his head a little harder. "Uh, did you need something?"

The man with the key chain was holding it up, almost like he was showing it off. This gave Alan a good enough view of it that he realized it wasn't a key chain at all. Not precisely, anyway. It might have been a fob, but if there were any keys involved, they were clutched in his hand. Instead, it was a teardrop-shaped piece of brilliantly gleaming silver. The faces of it were slightly flattened and had embossed designs that Alan couldn't quite place. He squinted at it. The thing caught the light in very distracting ways. It almost seemed to shine brighter than the light it was reflecting.

Run.

Alan looked to the man holding it.

"I'm sorry, but is that a Mason thing? Freemasons?"

The man with the fob seemed a bit distracted, eyes trained on the way it was shifting. It hung straight down and was lazily twisting back and forth. The ribbons of light it cast kept shining in Alan's eyes. It was growing quite irritating.

Run.

"Just... I just..." the man said.

From the way he was stalling and gazing at the fob, Alan got the distinct impression he was waiting for it to tell him something before he could proceed.

Alan looked back and forth between the two of them.

"Right, so—" *Run.* "I'm just going to be going—" *Run.* "I hope you guys have a great—" *Run.* "Day."

His heart was racing. The pair hadn't done anything overtly threatening, but they were giving him a terrible vibe. The taller man gave a silent nod to his shorter partner.

"Have you been feeling all right recently, sir?" said the man as he pocketed the key chain. "Trouble sleeping? Seeing things, maybe?"

"Uh... Listen, I'm sure you guys have some really good intentions, but I've got to go submit my shots for the day, so—"

Run, NOW! Run!

He felt a genuine, savage bolt of fear rip through him. He turned to find the second man had sidled around him and was pulling something gleaming from his pocket. In an instant, things went from a mildly irritating conversation with a couple of harmless weirdos to an attempted mugging in Alan's brain. Despite having lived in a big city his entire life, he'd never bothered to put together a contingency plan for this sort of thing. He panicked and did the first thing he could think of. He jumped back, cried out, and started snapping pictures.

The potent professional flash on his camera flickered again and again, dazzling the pair and making it clear that whatever they planned to do would be well documented. The stomping feet of people running up to investigate echoed through the parking structure. Instant evidence and witnesses.

The muggers hadn't planned for that reaction. One of them snatched at the camera. Alan pulled it back and defended it as though it were his child. As Good Samaritans rounded the corner, the muggers completely abandoned whatever their plan was. Both ran for all they were worth back the way they'd come.

Alan's vision was swimming, awash in faint purple stains from the flash rebounding off car headlights. Shadows shifted and twisted as cars must have rounded turns. The shorter of the fleeing muggers caught his foot on something dark and went sprawling onto the ground. The clank of metal echoed in the stark concrete structure. He scrambled to his feet and joined his partner in vanishing around a turn.

Just like that, it was over. The danger was gone.

"You okay, man?" asked one of the trio of travelers who had heeded his call.

Alan's pulse thumped in his ears. "Yeah. I'm fine. There was... did anyone see where they went?"

"Nah, man. They just ran off."

The three men and Alan worked their way through a stunted bit of post-trauma numbness. He exchanged information with one of them before they went on their way. Once they were gone, Alan didn't waste any time getting to the safety of his car.

He turned the key, but something nagged at him. He shut the engine back off.

"You know what?" he said. "I should report this. If you see something, say something. Those are the rules, right?"

He locked the door, just to be safe, and dialed the number for the police station.

Two hours later, Alan was finally home. The police had arrived and questioned him. They wrote up a report and gave him a case number, but he'd come away with the impression that the police weren't overly interested in the attempted assault. He emailed the photos and called to follow up when he first stepped through his door, but it was either too soon or too minor for them to give it much attention. He'd been tossed between two different departments before they assured him that they would contact him, not vice versa. Finally, he gave up and just called Jessie directly. As long as he was going to be talking to people at the police station without getting any results, he may as well be talking to a friend.

"So who was it? Sort of a gruff-voiced guy who slurs his *S*'s?" she asked.

"What? No, I've got the picture here, he was about my height, blond—"

"No, not the mugger. The guy who gave you the runaround on the phone a couple of minutes ago."

"Oh. Yeah, that sounds about right."

"Yeah, that's Jacobs. They took him off 911 because he didn't really consider anything an emergency unless someone was bleeding or turning blue."

"A real paragon of compassion."

"Eh, you spend enough years on the force you start to recalibrate what constitutes a 'major criminal event,'" she said. "You have no idea the sort of calls we get. A couple of days ago someone called because someone 'kept breaking in and unscrewing his light bulbs.'"

"So there's probably not going to be an investigation then."

"Our hands are a little full right now," she said. "Between the festival and... well, I assume you've seen it on Twitter or something."

"I've been busy too. What's in the papers?"

"There's this ridiculous public health scare. Two... no, three people turned up dead in their homes. No signs of break-in. The coroner couldn't determine a cause of death."

"Wait, I *did* hear about this. There *was* a cause of death, wasn't there?" He flipped through his phone. "Yeah, it's right here. It says SCA and apnea."

"Alan, that's doctor-talk for 'his heart stopped beating and he stopped breathing.' We don't know why that happened. Anyway, someone made some ridiculous claim about a water-borne infection or something, and now we're getting flooded with people afraid to drink their water."

"So it isn't the water?"

"Nope, ruled it out. The people were in entirely different parts of town. No one else had any symptoms, and the water tested clear. People die out of nowhere all the time. Nothing special about this set."

"... That really sets my mind at ease, Jessie."

"So, besides almost getting mugged, how did today go? Was it worth skipping out on your forensic photography interview?"

"Oh, yeah. A banner day. I got a picture of Clint Howard buying a Cinnabon."

"You rock star, you."

"Did they interview anyone else?"

"Just internal people. Most of the time we end up hiring from inside the force. One guy was promising. They're going to send him for certification."

"So that's that."

"Probably. Unless the guy washes out."

Alan thumped the desk.

"Don't beat yourself up. I'm sure you'll get another chance."

"I won't hold my breath." He thumped the desk again. "Damn it, Mr. Cox..."

"If you are so dead set on getting a job with the force, why didn't you just take the test to be a cop?"

"I don't know..." His eyes lingered on a photo of the robber. "It's kind of hard to find a job for a photographer that doesn't feel kind of pointless in the big picture. Unless you're taking pictures of war zones and starving children, it's hard to convince yourself you're doing any good."

"Oof. You're a little young to be feeling the weight of the world on your shoulders. And that doesn't answer the question about why you didn't just join the force instead."

He shrugged, not that she could see. "I still feel like taking pictures is the one thing I'm really good at."

"Fair enough. But listen, I'm still on the clock, I should get going."

"Yeah, of course. Thanks for taking the call. I'll talk to you later."

"So long."

He hung up and slumped into his office chair. His mind wandered in slow circles for a few minutes.

The knife.

Talking about the forensic photographer position sparked something in his mind. He'd *just* been a part of a crime. He knew precisely where a crime scene was.

Get the knife.

The man had dropped the knife, hadn't he? Alan could distinctly remember the sound of it hitting the ground. Maybe...

Get the knife and lock it up.

He stood. His freezer was empty. He had to go shopping anyway. Maybe he could swing by the airport again, take some pictures. It'd be good practice. And maybe he could find the knife. More evidence was always better, right? And it would be dangerous to leave it out there where someone else could find it and get hurt.

Alan grabbed his coat and headed out the door.

Alan trudged up the parking ramp of the airport parking lot. He was curious enough to return and see what he could find, but not curious enough to pay for hotel parking, so there was a *lot* of walking before he got back to the scene of the crime.

He didn't need to double-check that he'd found the right place again. Everything from the echo of his footsteps to the not-quite-bright-enough flickery light brought back memories of his brief encounter. He didn't think it had been terribly traumatic, but the closer he got to where his clash with the muggers had taken place, the more his heart started to flutter.

"Come on," he muttered. "You want to do this for a living. You can't be losing your nerve so easily."

Alan stalked through the parking area and kept his eyes trained on the ground. There were a surprising number of places for dropped objects to hide. Inside drains. Tucked into safety railings. Slid deep under any number of cars. He tried to be thorough, but after a half hour of searching, all the while with his mind nagging him about side hustles that he could be doing, he was just about ready to call it quits.

An odd flicker of motion caught his eye as he turned back to the ramp to head home. When he turned, all he saw was his shadow twisted across a curb beside a garbage can.

"I could *swear* I saw something," he murmured.

Alan crept closer to the trash. He was a little tense. As high strung as the return to the crime scene had gotten him, he was fairly certain something as startling as a rat jumping out of the trash would send him into cardiac arrest.

He reached the trash can without incident and nudged the trash. It rustled a bit more than physics would dictate. Something was underneath it. He pulled on an old glove and brushed the trash aside. Sure enough, camouflaged among some shiny potato-chip bags was the dagger.

Even among the muck and dust, the gloriously polished weapon remained bright and pristine. It certainly didn't look like the sort of thing a common mugger would use. The blade was just as highly buffed as the rest of their accessories had been. It also had many of the same vaguely cultish symbols embossed on it. The handle had the organic curl of something carved off an animal rather than a tree. An elk's horn, if he had to take a guess. He crouched to get a better look. While it certainly had the look of a dagger, it wasn't terribly sharp. The edges of the "blade" were blunt and rounded. The only remotely threatening part was the very tip, which with a bit of effort could probably draw blood.

"Did someone really just try to rob me with a letter opener?" he muttered to himself.

Alan's shadow slid aside. He hastily sidled closer to the trash can to avoid the approaching car. When it didn't go grinding past, he turned to find there was no car after all.

"Gotta finish this up. I'm way too jumpy right now."

He pulled a makeshift forensics kit from his pocket and laid it out. First, he positioned a little evidence marker, complete with size indicators. Then, he took some pictures from multiple angles. He considered calling the police again and seeing if they wanted to investigate further, but the thought of how much more of his day would get eaten by the wait, combined with the lackluster interest they'd taken in his attempted assault the first time, convinced him it was probably best just to bag it up and take it home.

Alan shook out a plastic zip-top bag he'd brought and carefully placed the blade inside.

Lock it up.

He slipped the bag into his spacious jacket pocket. It probably *was* a good idea to put it somewhere safe. Aside from the investigative potential it offered, the thing looked and felt rather valuable.

The job done, he packed up the rest of the kit and trotted back down the ramp to find his car.

A short time later, Alan loaded his fridge and freezer with as much bulk bargain-brand food as he could fit. Normally, he found the Tetris-ing of food in his undersized apartment fridge almost meditative, but the nagging little voice in his head hadn't shut up about the knife since he'd found it.

Lock it up somewhere. Get rid of it.

His jaw tightened. That was exactly what he would normally do. Just toss the thing somewhere out of the way and try to forget it. Alan had enough sources of anxiety. If this thing had him stressed, it should go. Because of his tiny apartment, he'd made throwing away stuff he didn't need almost a way of life. His sentiment was wrapped up in digital items these days. If it couldn't hang on a wall or sit on a hard drive, he tried not to get too attached. But something about this knife, the way the simple object seemed to have him so utterly on edge, chaffed him. And there was something in what Jessie had said earlier, too. If he wanted to make a difference, he should make a change.

He fetched and peeled open the bag that contained the knife. "If nothing else, I guess I'll figure out if I'm any good at investigation."

Largely working from things he'd seen in police procedurals, he dug out a ruler and dropped it on the desk beside the blade and adjusted the lighting for some detailed pictures. He wasn't sure what he'd achieve. It wasn't like he could dust it for prints. The most likely outcome would be him finding his way to an Amazon listing for a costume dagger. But it was something to do. If nothing else, it beat dwelling on the near attack that fell short of the police threshold for investigation.

Chapter 3

Alan shuffled forward a few steps and checked his watch. It was Sunday, and his investigation had proved even more ill-advised than he'd expected. If the knife *was* a cheap tchotchke, it sure wasn't a popular one. Mostly, he'd spiraled down a hole of trying to identify the symbols on it. After many hours, he'd concluded that they were an inaccurate mishmash of various religious and folkloric images all dealing with archetypal conflicts between good and evil. It had cost him several hours of sleep, and as he was now discovering, it was likely to cost him an awful lot more than that.

He'd overslept again. He'd never had a problem with it before, but now it seemed like his alarm just couldn't do the job. The assignment meeting pep talk was already over by the time he arrived, so the long line of people getting their index cards was already churning along. He'd hopped on right at the tail end. Not that it mattered. Being near the front hadn't exactly paid dividends yesterday.

When he finally made it to Cox, he had quite a few cards left in his hand.

"Fontaine. For a minute I thought you were a no-show. Lucky me you're good in the clutch." He slapped the entirety of the index cards into Alan's hand. "See if you can get something worthwhile out of that. I almost tossed them in the trash. The eyes were too big for the stomach."

Cox marched away without another word. From the speed in his stride, one would think he was trying to hurry away before Alan could say anything to him. That impulse had proved to be a wise one when Alan actually looked at the cards.

"What is this stuff..." he said, flicking through.

The so-called "photo-ops" he'd been assigned looked more like someone had just written down a list of places people might gather. Most of them were tourist traps. Two of the more popular cheesesteak places were there. City hall was too, for some reason. He'd even put the public library on the list.

"I guess I'll corner the market on superstar bookworms," he grumbled.

Alan stuffed the cards into his pocket and paced out into the hall. Marie-Anna was there, flipping through her meaty assignments and loading up the agenda on her phone. Her purse hung from her shoulder and was so stuffed with cards and credentials that she couldn't zip it. Alan had never stuck around late enough to be the last to leave, but knowing she'd mostly likely gotten her cards first made it a bit odd that she was still around. A more suspicious man might suggest she was waiting around for Cox to be done.

She glanced up from her phone and squinted at the glare from the sun pouring down the hallway. "Oh, hey."

Alan shifted so his shadow fell on her face, hoping to block the sun so she wouldn't have to squint at him. "Looks like you're in for a busy night," he said, pointing at her bag.

"Heh, yeah. Cox runs me ragged. I might have to pick and choose."

"If you're overbooked, I'd be happy to take some of your overflow." He flicked his own stack. "I'm pretty sure I'm not going to get any shots of Denzel Washington down at Geno's."

She gave a disingenuous smile. "Yeah, no. I think I got it."

"Shouldn't you get moving then? Or do you need a ride?"

She glanced up from her phone again. "No. Run along. I'm waiting here for a reason, and it doesn't involve or concern you."

The phrasing was brusque, but perhaps not entirely uncalled for. Alan had worked with this crew of photographers for a while, and he wouldn't put it past some of them to have made some vile propositions to her. She had no way of knowing that Alan wasn't that sort of guy. But for some reason the dismissive sweep she made with her hand to accompany the comment was enough to rile him just a bit. The moment passed quickly.

"Okay then. Have a good day," Alan said.

He paced back outside and found his way to his car. Once he was inside, he dug into his pocket and threw the index cards down on the seat beside him. He half considered just ditching them all and making the very reasonable claim the following day that no one of any tabloid value had shown up. Alas, even when it was the most intelligent decision, Alan couldn't bring himself to abandon an agreement.

The first step was to pull out his phone and check the budget. He had a monthly nut he had to hit, and with each passing month the amount of wiggle room was diminishing. Life had been reduced to "pictures per bill." Seven worthwhile photos for rent. Three for health insurance. Two for phone, cable, internet. It didn't sound like much, but it could be feast or famine. Sometimes a full day of shooting would only fetch him one sold photo, and he didn't get full shoots every day. This month he was running quite a deficit.

"Unless Alec Baldwin shows up and slugs a librarian, I don't think today's the day I'm going to finish funding room and board." He rubbed his neck. "Maybe I can book a wedding or something. Or an office party? I think that IT place threw a weird Thanksgiving party last year…"

He reached aside and picked up the index cards. Something slid from the pile and flopped onto the seat.

It wasn't an index card. It was the wrong shape for that. He plucked it up. The thing was a bit larger than an index card, made from some sort of thick, ornate stock, and vaguely resembled a wedding invitation. There was an awful lot of flowery language on it. "In honor of the people of Philadelphia" this and "with great gratitude for your generous contribution" that. It took him a few moments to register just what it was he was holding.

"This is… no… this is for the charity dinner." He flicked it. "This is a ticket for the big charity dinner!" He laughed with glee. "All the big names in local politics, some movie stars, and with anybody eager to be rubbing elbows with them. This is the kind of thing that'll make my *quarter*, let alone my month."

Alan paused and glared at the card. "There is no earthly way he meant for me to have this. There's no way it ended up buried in the bottom of the assignment stack. This is the sort of thing Jerry hands out separate. This is a mistake."

Keep it.

"I really shouldn't keep it. I should bring this back in. At least to make sure he knows—"

Forget the rules. Win for once.

55

The impulses were uncharacteristically potent. Sure, everyone has those little moments where they consider doing the easy thing, but typically these moments didn't make it front and center in his mind so readily. Still... if he *did* give himself the benefit of the doubt, this could really help him end the year with a firm footing, and maybe even illustrate to Cox what sort of work he could do under ideal circumstances. He grappled with the decision for five long, thoughtful minutes, then made his decision.

"I hope my suit still fits."

That evening, after a cursory visit to the other more official assignments he'd been given, Alan found himself at the front door of a restaurant he very much doubted he'd have ever set foot in if not for the ticket. Huge glass doors with polished brass hardware swung open to reveal the nearest thing that America had to a royal reception. Elegant tables circled what in other circumstances probably would have been a dance floor. Today the floor had another purpose. Before they even offered him his first flute of champagne, he made sure they knew he was press. In events like this, press was treated a little differently than the normal attendees. They took a lot more care checking identification, for starters. After that, they were wrangled into different positions for photo ops here or there, rather than being left to mingle with the crowd. And during those times when there weren't speeches or other planned publicity events, the media was shepherded around by a handler. It wasn't unlike being on a field trip.

"While the attendees enjoy the dessert course, allow me to show you the main fundraising opportunity for the evening," said an elegantly dressed woman speaking in her finest nonregional dialect. "Philadelphia is a city of considerable history."

She spread her arms magisterially toward the dance-floor display. It was filled with easels. Each displayed paintings, prints, and other art pieces fit for museum display.

"Local artisans were commissioned by the festival organizers to immortalize some of the more significant and meaningful moments in our fine city's past. All paintings are available for auction, with the proceeds going to fund a wing of a local children's hospital."

Cameras flashed, heads nodded, droning continued. This was actually the precise sort of thing Alan normally would have enjoyed. Where else would he find an oil painting of Sylvester Stallone and Burgess Meredith? But as fascinating as the actual good deeds that inspired the event were, using his potentially ill-gotten ticket and not getting any top-dollar images would make the whole enterprise pointless.

His impatience must have been properly calibrated, as not two minutes later he felt a tap on his shoulder. A rather greasy young man leaned forward to inspect Alan.

"You're a Cox man," he said.

"I beg your pardon?"

"You're who Cox sent?" the man clarified. "The official photographer?"

"Uh, well, I ended up with the ticket. You are?" Alan said, extending a hand.

"Davis. I'm his interviewer. I thought he'd send his chick for this sort of thing."

Alan shrugged and repeated, "I'm the one who ended up with the ticket."

It was the not-a-lie that he chose to latch on to, and he was going to stick with it until pressed. Fortunately (and not very encouragingly), the interviewer didn't have any further questions.

"Come on," Davis said. "The lineup starts over here. They're going to get rolling on the red-carpet-type stuff in about ten, and I want to get near the middle."

"Isn't the red carpet usually before the event?" Alan asked.

"That's why I said red-carpet-type. They're going to line people up to tag paintings they want to bid on. Now let's go. Does that thing do video?"

"Of course it does. Do you want to hook your mic up, or..."

"No, no. I'll send the files to Cox separate. He's got a post-prod guy for that. Come on, quit wasting time." He led the way over to a velvet rope at the head of the painting area, dictating his requirements. "Normally, there'd be another camera here to handle video photos, but Cox is—you're not shooting video yet, right?"

"Of course not."

"Cox is an idiot who treats assignments like gold stars to give to his favorites rather than actual jobs that need basic coverage. The guy can sell media like no one I've ever met, but I wish he'd get his hands on an assistant who actually understands talent. Anyway, that's neither here nor there. The point is, you're going to have to roll video and shoot photos."

"Not both at the same time, I hope."

"No, no. But give me a ten-second lead in and a ten-second lead out on the interviews, and every spare moment besides should be shooting either

B-roll or stills." He found his way to his chosen spot and gestured with his head.

"You should have plenty of time. Wayne there from the entertainment desk at the nightly news is a chatterbox. He'll keep folks two minutes longer than anyone else. Plenty of time for photos. I'm not on-camera talent, so frame me out, but..."

As Davis continued his instruction, a smile came to Alan's face. For the first time in too long, he was doing something that felt like it required his skills. He was a realist, so he tried to keep optimism reined in, but he couldn't help but feel like this was the start of a whole new chapter of his career.

"Great, great. Thanks for talking to us," Davis said, shaking hands.

Alan recorded the celebrity walking off and switched over to shooting some more photos. He couldn't believe his luck. So far he had a good twenty minutes of interview footage of celebrities ranging between the B- and C-list, which were a far better grade than he usually had to depend upon. It had taken a little bit of doing to rig up something that gave them the proper lighting, but now he had fallen into a tight little pattern of alternating photo and video that would easily be enough to fill two whole sections of a print paper and a couple of days worth of hourly posts on a news blog. And now his designated interviewer was getting ready to do the preliminary buttering up on the incumbent senator, Richard Savage. The front pages *loved* this guy. He was the platonic ideal of a traditional politician: dignified, at an indeterminate late-middle-age, a shock of silver coloring otherwise black hair, dressed in a suit that looked well-tailored and sharp without being showy or extravagant, and able to talk for minutes at a time without taking any firm position. Against all odds, he'd managed to rise above the general cesspool that had consumed most of local politics to retain his respect among the community.

Mostly. No one was entirely free from scandal, and as Alan switched to video and Davis lobbed some softballs, a specific line of questioning reared its ugly head.

"What do you think of the recent claims by your opponent, Senator Savage?" Davis asked.

"I can only speak in glowing terms of the distinguished Arthur Magnuson. His record as the commissioner of our fair police force speaks for itself. I take it on good faith that he trusts his sources. Unfortunately, I think he is being led astray, and I'm confident further investigation will confirm that."

"Insider trading is a serious charge."

"Indeed it is, and one that should not be spuriously applied, which is why, again, I am confident further investigation will confirm my innocence."

Davis continued down the rather hard-hitting line of questioning. Alan would have thought a more sanitized, impact-free collection of questions would have been called for in the case of a charity event, but he supposed that was why he was the one with the camera instead of the microphone. Currently, his greater concern was the fact that a younger man shadowing the senator, presumably an intern, had terrible media instincts. He glanced in Alan's direction almost constantly, often staring down the barrel of the camera in a terribly amateur way. Every time a flash from a nearby photo happened, he flinched slightly. Alan had to work to frame him out of the shot.

"Well I hope you find a painting you like, Senator."

"I'm sure I will. Thanks for your great questions," Savage said, his winning smile not once leaving his face.

They shook hands and the night rolled on. In his mental tally, Alan rolled over from "barely squeaking by" to "possibly knocking off some credit card debt" over the course of several hours. Once the interviews were over and the handlers were done directing the cameras to this or that, he was free to rove the perimeter of the event and take some more subdued, careful photos. As the night was winding down, he decided to take some B-roll. In his experience, the people who put together video packages for an event like this always liked to have those little filler scenes. He caught some video of waiters handing out champagne, followed by a shot of the auctioneer banging his gavel and pointing out a winner. He was just filming a nice slow pan of the crowd gathered outside the building in preparation for the departure of the guests when a familiar, irritating glare swept across his camera.

He pulled his head away from the viewfinder to look the crowd over. It was a press of people, pushed so close together it was hard to make people out as individuals. The security the organizers had hired to keep the path clear didn't make it any easier, constantly stepping into view to wrangle people. Finally, he saw it again, a glint from somewhere in the crowd. He raised the camera and zoomed. A hand was raised up above the rest of the crowd, dangling a polished silver teardrop. It was precisely the same as the one his would-be mugger had brandished. He zoomed in and lingered on the piece. He couldn't see the person holding it, only an arm that disappeared behind the rest of the crowd. Was it possible that this was the same person who had tried to rob him? Surely not. Surely this was just a similar pendant. But for a moment he was bothered less by the presence of the pendant and more by its behavior. Despite the jostle of the crowd, the pendant stayed rock solid, never losing its alignment. It faced the restaurant, not even angling away when the man holding it twisted his hand to wrap it back into his palm and vanished entirely into the crowd.

Alan's mind locked on to the curiosity so intently he nearly failed to notice that the wrap-up was well underway. If he wasn't careful, he'd miss out on the prime photo ops of the departure.

After the charity event was done, he did another quick circuit of the other lackluster assignments he'd been given. It yielded another picture of Clint Howard, this time buying a stuffed pretzel at Reading Market. Alan would say this of the guy: he knew a good snack when he saw it. Once he was satisfied he'd done his due diligence for the day, Alan ended the day as he often did: with a hastily made salad, some not-too-distracting music, and his laptop. He'd dropped the photos into the Cox Media share and was waiting for the videos to upload. He tried not to dwell on the fact that Cox had replied to the upload with the comment "Thanks Babe :*". At the moment, his greater interest was on the research project he'd had to set aside until now. The knife he'd found and its possible origins.

The amount and nature of his searches had probably added his name to a few watch lists, as the more he dug into the images, the more they led him to places that pretty clearly qualified as the nebulously defined dark web. All of the images that came close to matching the exact configuration of symbols on the blade directed back to a small cluster of sites referencing the same sort of thing. It was either a bunch of different cults or one big one with a bunch of different names. For the most part, the names sounded like they'd been rejected by a screenwriter trying to rip off *Game of Thrones*. They included such gems as The Slicers of the Darkness, Gleaming Silver, and Lone Beacons. Who precisely decided pluralizing something that was supposed to be "lone" probably needed to brush up on their grammar. The most common name appeared to be The Dawn. It was either a coincidence or a devilish bit of cleverness, but that was where his research stopped. There was no reasonable way to search for a group named The Dawn without getting a boatload of useless search results about the time of day.

"Ugh..." he grumbled. "I need a drink."

He stood and trudged toward the kitchen. After a moment, he decided to grab the dagger and bring it with him.

"I wonder if I emailed Jessie what I found, if she could tell me more. Nah. I already flaked on the interview she set up. The last thing I need is to drive her nuts with this cult nonsense. Probably, it's just a letter opener someone found at a pawn shop or an estate sale."

He hefted the weapon in his hand while he waited for his coffee machine to finish dripping out a pot. One of those single-serving machines would be a heck of a lot more convenient. But on a per-cup basis—particularly with the amount of coffee he drank—he just couldn't justify the cost.

He hefted the dagger again. "Feels heavy. I wonder if this is solid silver. Heh. That'd be a kick if somebody tried to steal five thousand dollars worth of camera with ten thousand dollars worth of dagger."

The coffee finished and he poured a cup. He debated heading back to his desk to dig a little deeper, but the fruitless research was starting to give him a headache. He decided the better course of action would be to turn on the TV and turn off his brain for a while. He turned to the couch, which by virtue of his tiny apartment was only a few strides from his kitchen. The living room had no lights on, so his shadow stretched across the whole room, cast only by the faint light of the oven's vent hood. His cheap but comfortable couch was calling his name, so he strolled toward it and lobbed the dagger in a lazy arc toward the seat so he could free up a hand to reposition the pillows. When he tossed it, the couch was almost entirely eclipsed by his shadow. When it landed, the light of the kitchen reflected off the blade and glared in his eyes.

It took him another step forward before the inconsistency struck him. He turned to the light. It was directly behind him. He turned to the couch, his shadow was off to the side.

"What kind of wacky... where's that light coming from if not..."

He waved his hand. His shadow did the same. He stepped aside, his shadow followed him. He reached his shadowy hand toward the blade.

His shadow hesitated.

"What the hell..." he muttered.

Alan marched closer, purposely trying to get his shadow to overlap the blade, but it skewed aside like someone was moving the light behind him. But that *couldn't* be happening. It was a stationary fixture. When he was close enough, he leaned down to snatch up the dagger. His shadow shuddered and twitched around the shadow of the knife, like they were matching poles of a magnet he was trying to hold together. He maneuvered himself so that his shadow was cast on a wall in front of him and stepped up to it, dagger in hand. As he got closer, the whole outline of the shadow quivered and trembled. Slowly, he moved the knife closer to the shadow. It was six inches away. Three inches. One inch.

White slits, precisely where the eyes should be, slid open on the shadow, then a thin white maw that quickly widened into a terrified grimace.

"Don't!" it shrieked, its voice more in his head than his ears.

If his mind was still functioning clearly, he might have realized he recognized the voice. But any thought of that kind was entirely lost in the far more potent commands of the much vaunted fight or flight reflex. In Alan's case, it was typically just the flight reflex. That survival mechanism was not evolved with a small apartment in mind. He turned, accelerated to a full sprint in three strides, and came to a dead stop in one punishing impact with the kitchen doorway. Blue and red sparks filled his vision, the knife bounced off the wall, his coffee splattered to the kitchen floor, and he crumbled to the ground in a daze.

The room spun and churned around Alan as his brain tried to untangle itself from the impact. A dull throb in his forehead drew his attention first. He reached up to find he'd earned a nice knot just at the hairline. He blinked away some tears and tried to raise his head, but the room's slow waver and rotation accelerated briefly as he did so, causing his stomach to lurch threateningly. He took it as a sign that he should probably stay down for a bit longer.

His slowly returning wits began to assert certain observations. Setting aside the inexplicable event that had sent him barreling into the wall in the first place, he was quite certain he had landed on the floor. Now he was resting somewhat awkwardly on the couch. And then there was the fact that his view of the ceiling featured his shadow. Unless his couch was glowing, there was no physical explanation for such a thing. The last and to a large degree the most important observation he made was that his shadow still had the same white eyes gazing down at him from above.

Some very pressing questions came to mind, but his mouth was not up to the task of coherently rendering them, so he decided to start with something simple.

"How?"

There was no reply. The white eyes simply blinked once then shut, rendering the shadow a featureless silhouette once more.

"I saw you," he slurred. "You aren't fooling anyone."

Still no reply. He risked sitting up again, and this time managed to teeter to a sitting position. The shadow shifted around and ended up beside him on the couch, which was precisely where it should have been based upon the actual lighting. He felt over the darkened section of couch, but there was nothing there. Just the rough fabric of the seat cushion.

"No..." he said, shaking his head slowly to avoid stirring up his dizziness. "I know I saw what I saw. And heard what I heard. You're not going to gaslight me."

He scanned the room and spotted the dagger. When he'd struck the wall, the dagger had fallen from his hand. In retrospect, he was lucky that his clumsy dash with a weapon in his hand hadn't ended with the mostly blunt thing jabbed into his thigh. As it was, the only consequence was a terrible mess of coffee on the kitchen floor and a gouge in his drywall. He held tight to the arm of the couch and extended his leg to try to sweep the knife closer. When he nudged it with his toe, the shadow stretching across the floor briefly separated from his foot and gingerly nudged the knife out of reach.

"Okay, I saw that!" he snapped.

He slid to the floor and crawled toward the knife. Each time he reached for it, the shadow nudged it just a bit more to push it out of range. Finally, he heaved himself forward and snatched the weapon up. The shadow instantly peeled away from his crawling form, pressing itself against the far wall with only a thin ribbon of darkness connecting itself to his feet. He rolled to his back and brandished the dagger like he was training a gun on the trembling silhouette.

"Please! Don't! I beg you, put it down!" his shadow insisted.

The shape gradually changed. It became shorter and a bit stouter. Flowing hair roiled up from its head. Around its edge was the hint of dangling rags. It was still a shadow, a "normal" one if one ignored the eyes and mouth, but it was no longer *his* shadow. But for the moment the bizarreness of the vision before him was forced aside by the dim flicker of recognition.

"You're... you are the girl from the dreams."

The shadow shifted in a way that may have been crossing its arms. "I am. Yes! I am! And remember how I helped you? I helped with the homework, and I opened the door for you. I'm your *friend*. You wouldn't pull a knife on your friend!"

He rubbed his head and winced as he brushed across the lump. "Am I dreaming now?"

The eyes narrowed. "Yes. Yes, this is a dream. Another very strange dream and that knife isn't even a real knife anyway. It is a dream knife. So you may as well put it down. Carefully." She pointed. "Over there."

He wrestled himself up on his elbows. Doing so swept the knife about a bit. The shadow trembled and forced itself into the corner.

"By the void, would you be careful with that thing?!"

"For a dream talking to a dreaming man with a harmless dream knife you seem awfully concerned about it." He probed the throbbing lump on his head again and came away with a dab of blood. "And I don't know that I've ever felt pain quite this realistic in a dream."

"How would you know? You barely remember dreams."

"And how would *you* know that I barely remember dreams?"

"Because I'm a dream! Who better to know how you dream than your dream?"

He shook his head. "No. This doesn't make any sense."

"Exactly why this is a dream. Dreams don't make sense. See? Your logic, not mine."

"Enough with this dream nonsense."

He rolled over and started to climb laboriously to his feet. It was hard enough to do with his equilibrium randomly disagreeing with him. Having the knife in his hand made it harder still. When he finally tottered to his feet, he promptly lost grip of the blade, and it thunked tip-first into the carpet. The weight and point were enough for it to pin itself lightly.

His shadow screeched. The point had driven itself right into the thin band of shadow being cast from him. Her cries were genuine pain, and her shape darted and shuddered across the wall. Slashing, waving hands caused photos on his wall to swing and shift like they were being batted about by a powerful breeze. Her white mouth and eyes were wide with terror.

Alan's confusion and anger instantly fell aside in the wake of the surge of empathy he felt. The pain and fear were so genuine, every fiber of his being demanded that he put it to an end. He hastily snatched up the knife, pulling it from the floor and tossing it onto the end table.

"It's okay! It's gone now. I pulled it out. I'm sorry! I'm sorry! That was an accident."

His shadow, still shaking, calmed down. She slid down off the wall and across the floor, huddling over the point where the blade had struck. There was a thin but noticeable gap in the shadow, like someone had sliced a small slit in a sheet of paper. She gingerly touched it much as he'd been testing his head injury.

"It wasn't an accident," she said. "You did that on purpose. I asked you to be careful and you did that anyway." She sounded genuinely hurt, and not just physically.

"Look, I'm sorry, but this is all new to me. I don't know what's going on." He furrowed his brow. "Wait, why am I apologizing to you? You're lurking in my shadow."

She sniffed. "I didn't *stab* you."

"Just... what *are* you? What is this about?"

His shadow turned her back on him, a motion mostly discernible thanks to her eyes sliding around and out of sight.

"I'm not telling you anything. You don't scare me. And do you know why?"

"No, I don't! I don't know *anything* about this."

"It's because you can't get rid of me. We're linked, Alan. You need me as much as I need you."

"What are you talking about?"

"You can't live without a shadow, and *I'm* your shadow. If you try to slice me off, you sign your own death warrant." She waggled a finger. "So don't you even try it."

"That doesn't make any sense. I can't *not* have a shadow. That's physics."

"You can now. That's metaphysics." She turned back to him, a devilish curve to her eyes and smirk on her lips. "You want proof?"

"I'd like anything that answers some questions."

She nodded and huffed. "Just remember what this feels like."

The shadow spread her somewhat stubby arms. As she did, they extended. Though the word barely seemed appropriate, the way the shadow shifted and elongated seemed perfectly natural. Shadows were mutable things, growing and shrinking, stretching and skewing. He could have easily imagined that what he saw on the wall was the result of a clever bit of positioning in front of a light. Shadow puppetry. The only difference was that it was happening with his own shadow while he watched in silent confusion. Her fingers grasped the shadow of the couch, then the shadow of the entertainment center on the other side. After another breath, she pulled away. One foot peeled away from his own with agonizing slowness. As it did, there was an undeniable sensation. He didn't have the words to describe it. The feeling was unlike anything he'd experienced before. His leg started to feel... empty. *False*, even. As the other foot started to pull away, some sense of self, some sense of *reality* started to drain away from him. It was like he was steadily losing his humanity, like the vivid colors were draining from his being and little more than a husk was being left behind. His existence was a kite, and someone had released the string.

Her other foot snapped away from him. Alan shivered. He knew, down to his core, that he no longer belonged. Not here, not anywhere. The world no longer had a place for him. His shadow, or the creature that had come to replace it, hung on the wall now. She was unconnected to him. From the look of her, she was feeling much the same thing as he was, but in a far more fundamental way. Her outline quivered and danced. Her fingers dug deep into the furniture. Ghostly dimples, then deep punctures appeared on the arm of the couch as she held tighter. Deep gouges into the veneer curled up. Finally, she could take it no longer, and she thrust her feet back toward his. Relief rushed over them both. Alan released a breath he'd not realized he was holding. It curled in the air before him as though he'd been in the iciness of winter. A numbness of the soul eased away.

"That's everything you need to know about me," she said hoarsely. "You need a shadow, and I'm the only one you've got."

"You can't just... after that... I *need* to know more. You've got to answer some questions."

"I don't have to do anything," she said. "You are a terrible host. All I've done is try to help you and you stabbed me."

She shifted across the room and plopped onto the shadow of the couch with an unmistakably pouty posture. Alan went to palm his forehead and rediscovered the throbbing lump he'd earned. He winced and thumped out into the kitchen. A heady mix of confusion, frustration, helplessness, and shame ratcheted his anxiety levels up as he rummaged through his freezer for something to take the swelling down. He fetched an ice pack he used for his lunches and slapped it on the counter to crunch it up, then held it to his head. He shut the freezer door and jumped as his white-eyed shadow showed up on the wall beside him.

"What about me?"

"What *about* you?" he said.

"You're treating *your* wound." She pointed to her leg, which still had the odd sliver of light shining through her thigh where the knife had landed. "What about me?"

He sucked a breath through his teeth, squinting at the injury. "I didn't... that must have really hurt."

"You have no idea."

"What do I do? Is there... like... a shadow bandage?"

"No. I just need to heal. But that helps."

She pointed to the cup of coffee spilled all over the floor. He raised an eyebrow and glanced at her incredulously. "Coffee helps you heal?"

"Well I *like* coffee. It will make me feel better."

He opened a cabinet and fetched a roll of paper towels. After laying out enough of them to soak up the worst of the spill and swishing them around with his foot, he grabbed a fresh mug and filled it from the pot.

"How long have you been here?" he asked.

She didn't answer.

"You're the one who's been whispering all that bad advice, aren't you?"

"It wasn't bad advice," she replied defensively. "If you'd run when I told you to run, it would have been better for both of us. Do you know how close we came to ending up dead?"

"So you know who those guys are?"

She turned to him and put her hands on her hips. "Yes! *Them* I'll tell you about, just so you know to stay away."

"Okay, so who are they?"

"They're..." She paused, hand gesturing vaguely in the air. "Well, I don't know what *you'd* call them, but they're a secret group. They're a group who *thinks* they know about people like me. They want to *kill* people like me. Which means now they're people who want to kill people like you."

"Why?"

"Because you've got me now."

"But why do they want to kill you?"

"As if you don't know."

"If I knew I wouldn't be asking!"

"Because we're darkness, that's why!" She pointed at the light bulb. "Don't pretend like your people haven't dedicated your lives to wiping out the darkness."

"Darkness isn't alive."

She gestured to herself. "Pieces of it are! But you don't care, do you? All you want to do is chase us into little corners. You don't care about balance. You want nothing but light."

"Never in my life have I seen a shadow move and think on its own. If I had, I would probably act differently."

"The fact that you've never seen one of us just proves it. This *isn't* the first time we've come here."

He looked to her. "You've come here. You're from somewhere else?"

Her eyes widened slightly as she realized what she'd said. "You won't weasel any more information out of me."

"You're not exactly building any bridges calling me a weasel," he said. He swirled the coffee in the cup. "How do you take it?"

"However I can get it."

"But, do you want sugar, cream?"

"How do you take it?"

"Black."

She nodded vigorously. "Like that."

He made ready to hand it to her. Almost immediately, the flaw in this plan became evident to him. For the moment at least, she was imitating his position as a shadow *should*, so her fingers were hooked through the handle of the mug's shadow just as his were holding the real cup.

"How do I..."

"Just let go," she said.

Doubtfully, he set the mug on the counter, then released it. His shadow did not, and after a bit of visible effort on her part, the mug lifted from the counter. It bobbed in the air precisely where it would have to be to cast its present shadow, but the figure holding it existed *only* in silhouette against the wall. He waved his hand through where an unseen figure would have had to be standing to hold it so, but there wasn't even the vague chill of a ghostly presence that he imagined he might feel. She put the cup to her lips and sipped at it delicately. In the dim light, he could see the ripple of the coffee and even the odd disruption of a pair of lips against the edge of the liquid, but there wasn't any sort of invisible-man-style tendril tracing out an invisible esophagus. The coffee just vanished.

She sighed pleasantly. "That's nice..."

"Where does it *go*?" he asked.

She looked haughtily to him. "Don't worry about where it goes."

He set up another mug to prepare himself a coffee and briefly grappled with how readily this had slipped from "supernatural happening" to "simple hospitality." It didn't feel alien or invasive, having her here. Maybe that meant she'd been with him for a very long time. Maybe it just meant it was nice to not be alone in the apartment for once. He watched as she nursed her coffee. For the most part, she was cradling the mug with both hands. At her somewhat diminutive size—he estimated that to cast a shadow her height, a person would be about four feet tall—the mug was just a tad large for her grip. She risked a single grip for a moment and ran her fingers through the hair that danced and waved around her head. Her eyes shut to little crescent moons, and she breathed in the scent of the coffee. She may have acted indignant, but she had the air of someone with badly rattled nerves desperate for a respite.

He knew the feeling.

"So you're not going to enlighten me about what this is all about?"

"You rammed yourself into a wall when you first saw me, and played with a knife when I warned you not to. I don't think you can handle the answers to the sort of questions you're asking. Not yet."

He took his coffee, held the ice pack to his head again, and paced from the room. She slid along the walls, the coffee cup drifting beside him.

"You realize I'm going to have to try to work it out on my own, then."

"You do what you think you have to do," she said. "But don't expect any help from me."

Long into the night, Alan sat at his laptop and tried to find some explanation for what was happening besides insanity or drug-induced hallucination. True to her word, his shadow refused to do anything beyond drink her coffee and slide along the wall in the glow of the laptop screen.

"These are... photographs, yes?" she said, viewing his little gallery.

"Yeah," he said without looking. "You know about them?"

"Not really. Not much." She dangled the empty coffee cup on one finger, now having much less difficulty carrying it. "Do you need to visit these places to take these photographs?"

"Of course."

The fingers of her free hand slipped across the front of a desert scene, tracing the shadow of a cactus stretching across the canvas.

"You didn't try to destroy these shadows..."

"I don't try to destroy shadows," he said. "Shadows are a big part of my composition. You've got to have some shadow to balance the highlights."

"Yes!" she said eagerly. "That's right! For every light a shadow. For every day a night. Is that so difficult to understand?"

Alan leaned aside to the lamp and clicked it on. His shadow yelped and snapped across the room to project on the opposite wall. The mug she'd been holding followed her at an uncontrollable speed. It hurled at the wall and shattered.

"*Warn* me when you are going to do something like that!" she snapped angrily.

"Sorry! I didn't know that would happen!" he said, turning to look at her on the wall while he adjusted the recently replaced ice pack.

"Don't pretend you don't know how shadows work. You couldn't make those photographs if you didn't know how shadows work." Her tone was fuming. As she spoke, she held her hand to her head.

"What's wrong? Did you hurt yourself?"

"No."

"Then why are you holding your head?"

"I'm not holding my head. You're holding *your* head."

He raised his other hand. She imitated. "Why are you doing everything I do now?"

"The light's too bright. I can't help it."

"Oh. *Oh*. Is that how it works?"

"Obviously."

He grabbed the camera off his desk and fiddled with some settings.

"You aren't going to use the light on that, are you?" she asked, the waver of fear in her voice.

"No. No flash. I want a shot of you."

He clicked a batch of pictures, then brought them up on his preview. Sure enough, there was the flowing-haired shadow, complete with its stark white eyes and frowning white mouth.

"Ha!" she said. "Proof!"

A sudden slam at his door startled him into nearly dropping his camera.

"Mr. Fontaine!" bellowed an all-too-familiar voice.

He hurried to the door of his apartment and pulled it open, camera still in hand. The bright light of the hallway cast his shadow straight and rigidly back behind him.

"What are you doing in here? Do you know what time it is? You can't just be slamming into walls and breaking glass. Some people are trying to—"

"Ms. Levitt, good!" he said, wild-eyed. "Can you look there and tell me what you see?" He pointed behind him, at his shadow.

"It's your apartment. Are you on drugs right now?"

"No, the shadow, is there anything off about the shadow?"

He glanced over his shoulder. The shadow was glaring back at him, imitating his position.

"It's a shadow. What happened to your head?"

"Fine, fine, here." He pulled up the camera and zoomed in on the shadow. "Here. Do you see that?"

"... It's your *shadow*."

"No, no. Right here." He zoomed until the unnatural eyes and mouth practically filled the preview screen.

"It's. Your. Shadow. Listen, Fontaine. The superintendent will be hearing about this. I refuse to live next door to a junkie."

She stormed away, disappearing back into her apartment while muttering under her breath. He shut the door and turned to his shadow. Without the bright light of the hall, only the dim light of the kitchen cast her. She slid up along the wall and glared at him.

"You'd better watch yourself," she fumed.

"So I guess other people can't see you."

"No, they can't. And it's a lucky thing, too. Or did you already forget that if something happens to me, something happens to you? And you'd better believe if word spreads that you've got a shadow like me, something is going to happen to me."

"But how... If I can see you and she can't, how would the cup thing work? And the... I've got more testing to do..."

The next hour was far more scientific than those that had come before. While his tight-lipped shadow glared at him, he spent time testing every aspect of her bizarre nature that he could think of. Moving the light, moving himself, attempting to interact with parts of her with the shadows of other things. Aside from some indignant grunts now and again, nothing he did suggested she was any different from a standard shadow, save the face and difference in shape that no one else could see. He jotted down notes and became increasingly concerned that all of this might be in his head. To set his mind at ease, he went and snapped pictures of the damage that had been done to his couch and entertainment center.

"Maybe different color lights? Does that make a difference?" he muttered. "I wonder if I have any gels I can use..." He stood and walked to his closet, placing him quite near the shadow's face.

"I don't care how much more you torture me, I won't say a word," she hissed at him.

He froze. "Torture? No, no. This isn't... that's not what I was doing. Is this unpleasant to you?"

"I can't *move*. How would *you* like it?"

"Oh my gosh, I'm so sorry. I wasn't thinking. This is. Hold on, I can't dim the lamp."

He pulled open the closet and found an old red bandanna that he threw over the lamp. The room eased down into a warm red glow, and immediately his shadow abandoned his pose for a sulking, cross-armed pout.

"About time," she stated.

"If you don't tell me how I'm supposed to treat you, how am I supposed to know?" he said. "I didn't hurt you, did I?"

"You mean before or after the stabbing?"

"You know what I mean. The light doesn't hurt, does it?"

"I... no, it doesn't. At least not as painful as you *thought* it was."

"I didn't think it was painful at *all*. I was just trying to learn." He adjusted the makeshift shade. "Listen, I don't know if this is pride or orders or whatever, but from now on if I'm hurting you, you let me know."

"Fine."

"Good," he said.

He turned back to his computer and started typing in his findings. She slid over to the wall beside him.

"What is it like then?" he asked.

"What, when the light is too bright?"

"Yeah. Is it... I don't know, like being tied up? Is that the only thing?"

"No, it's..." She grappled with herself for a moment. "It isn't all bad. It's... bracing, I guess. Like a bucket of cold water dropped over you. When the light is bright, I'm focused." She snapped her fingers. "Like that. It takes lots of effort to move at all. More strength than I have. But it takes zero effort to just *be*."

"So when the light's dim, you have to work just to exist?"

"It's... you wouldn't understand, Alan. You're always the same shape. We're not. It's the difference between holding your arm up and resting your arm on something."

A thought drifted through his head. "Can you... can you read my mind?"

She rolled her eyes. "I *wish*. I get things from you, but it's all very simple. Words. Notions. And it's hard to pick through them. I get what I get. Mostly, it just helped me catch up to how you speak, more or less. And half of that makes no sense. There's an awful lot of stuff that comes seeping out of your mind that isn't even remotely true."

She slid up until she was stretched on the desk below the lamp. "For instance, is this thing called a laptop?" she asked.

"Yeah."

"Why? It's on a desk. It should be a desktop."

"A desktop is something else."

"Why can't they both be a desktop?"

"So people can tell them apart I guess." He yawned. "Look, can we keep this on you for a second? We've barely scratched the surface and it's already... *4 a.m.!* I've got to get to bed. My alarm is going to go off in a couple of hours."

He flipped down the screen of his laptop and stood, then froze.

"Uh... can I get some privacy please?"

"Nope," she said simply.

"I have to get undressed, though. And in the morning I'll have to shower."

"So I've noticed."

Embarrassment burned in his chest, and his cheeks blushed deeply as he realized it had been at least a day or two since he'd started hearing the "devil on his shoulder" speak up, which meant she'd been through his daily routine with him a few times.

"That's... uh... I didn't..."

"What's the problem?" she said impatiently.

"I mean... you seem female, but do shadows even have gender?"

She gave him a hard look. "Listen, I may *be* your shadow, but I'm not just a shadow. Where I come from is a lot like where you come from, more or less, and thus we have the same spectrum of genders as you. And yes, I'm a woman, thank you very much."

"... This is going to be awkward."

"Don't be a prude."

"It's going to make me uncomfortable! I mean, were you watching me in the shower?"

"No. I had my eyes closed. You'd have noticed them if I hadn't."

"My shadow still looked like me until a few hours ago. You could have just been disguising yourself."

"I may be able to change my shape, but I can't see with my eyes shut."

"... Still."

She huffed. "So keep the light dim and I'll wait outside."

"No! You don't mean peeling off me, do you? That was..." He shuddered. "I didn't like that."

"Oh my darkness, of course not! I'll just, well, you just watch."

She pivoted herself around and cast herself upon the floor, then slid along, elongating herself until she was mostly out of the room. She then reached down, grabbed the shadow of the door, and tugged it shut. Rather than being cast on the door itself, she remained on the other side, like she was a black cutout that had been tucked under it.

"Tell me when you're done. This takes a little bit of effort," she said.

It was odd, her voice was still clear in his ears, not muffled through the door. But then, he supposed she couldn't very well have been talking out loud, she didn't have the right anatomy for it. But then, she didn't have the right anatomy for drinking coffee either...

He shook off the contradictions for now and pulled open his dresser. Clearly things that had been impossible that afternoon were suddenly quite real. There was going to be a calibration process before he could start making firm statements about reality again. Unless he woke up in the morning and found this whole ridiculous enterprise to be a dream. Somehow, he guessed that was far too much to hope for.

Typically, he slept in his underwear, but in light of the current situation, he opted for pajamas. When he was dressed, he called to her.

"Okay, we're good."

She snapped back into the room and hung on the wall vaguely where the light suggested she should be. He slid into bed and pulled up the covers. She remained on the wall. Gazing down at him.

"Do you sleep?"

"Not in the way you think of it."

"So you're just going to hang there and watch me?"

"Of course not. I'll join you in your dream, as I have before. If nothing else, it will help me learn a bit more about you."

"Dreams are supposed to be private."

"And shadows are supposed to be mindless. Things are going to be different from now on, Alan. Best to start getting used to it."

He gently tested the lump on his head. The swelling had gone down a bit. By morning it should just be a rotten bruise.

"I don't really have time to argue. Good night... I guess I don't know your name yet."

"Blot," she said. "My name is Blot."

"Good night, Blot. I hope you'll understand if I say I hope you turn out to be just a dream."

"Trust me, Alan, you wouldn't have been my first choice either."

83

JOSEPH R. LALLO

He lowered his faintly throbbing head to his pillow and slid into an
exhausted sleep.

Chapter 4

The following morning was a bit of a mixed bag. On the positive side of the equation, the lump on his head was now just a nasty bruise. And though he'd only slept a few hours, it had been a deep, glorious, black sleep. He didn't feel quite as much like a zombie as he'd expected. On the other hand...

"This stuff is divine... It makes me feel so powerful," Blot said, breathing deep over the shadow of her cup.

His shadow had stubbornly refused to return to its silent, stationary state. Right now she was sitting, aligned roughly with a chair at his table. The kitchenette didn't have any windows, so the soft light of the oven hood was gentle enough for her to freely roam the room. He'd managed to wrestle himself out of bed on his first actual alarm, meaning he had time for a real breakfast after a shower spent with his shadow waiting impatiently outside the room.

"It takes a cup of it to make me feel human in the mornings," Alan said, stirring at some scrambled eggs in a pan. "So do you eat? Should I be making you breakfast?"

Blot shook her head. "Not really. I *can*. But no thank you. I probably wouldn't have tried this stuff if not for how nice it smelled."

"I spotted you in the dream, by the way," he said.

"Well I wasn't going to *hide*. There's no reason for it anymore. That game you were playing looked silly, by the way."

"Oh, come on. Basketball is excellent. I used to be pretty good in high school."

"What were the fancy people on the side doing?"

"Fancy people..." He dumped the eggs onto a plate and ground some pepper onto them. "Oh, the cheerleaders?"

"Cheerleaders..." She nodded. "I thought for *sure* they would finish summoning whoever they were summoning before that game ended."

"Summoning. I think you're confused. They were just trying to get the crowd worked up."

Blot set her mug down with a click. "'Give me an *E*'? 'We've got spirit, yes we do'? They were making invocations for gifts from the great beyond. And they were *very* enthusiastic. Add some incense and some of the right runes and you'll get all the spirit you can handle."

"That's a weird thought." He sat down and picked up his fork. "I've been thinking."

"You do that a lot. You should do more acting and less thinking. That would serve us much better."

"I don't know that you're actually real."

"I'm real. Not in the way you people define the word. But I'm as real as your old shadow. More so, in fact, since it's gone."

"Don't think we're not going to discuss *that*, but right now, there's the issue of whether or not you exist. I'm the only one who has ever seen you."

"That's how it works."

"It's a little convenient, don't you think?"

"Your neighbor heard the mug smash on the wall."

"I could have thrown it myself."

"You'd remember if you did that."

"Not if I were crazy. You, and all of this, could be a figment of my imagination. How do I know my perception isn't faulty and all of this isn't really the way it seems?"

"How do you know your whole life *before* this wasn't the faulty part? At some point you've got to trust your senses."

"Look, if there was *anything* you did that someone else witnessed, I'd be more convinced."

"So you trust what other people see more than what you see?" She shook her head and picked up her mug again. "You're going to take a lot of work."

"For what?"

"To make you into a proper host."

"Oh, am I not living up to my end of the bargain I had no choice in?"

"Don't you want to be powerful and respected and revered? Or have lots of money? It seems like all you ever worry about is money."

"I'd like to have an easier time making ends meet, that's for sure."

"Well, me? I want influence. And I can't get any of my own. So it behooves me to help *you* get some. My life gets better if your life gets better, so I'm going to work just as hard as I can to make you a force to be reckoned with." She sipped her coffee. "I'm a *blessing*."

Alan raised an eyebrow. "I guess there's some logic to that. But, then, you could just be my subconscious trying to justify raw, unbridled ambition."

"Oh? And did your subconscious stuff sixty dollars in the pocket of your pants?"

He chewed on the words for a moment. "Wait. *That's* where that money came from?"

"Your awful neighbor was going to cost you the money for parking, or whatever it was. So I balanced the scales by grabbing some money from her." She swirled the coffee. "It's weird that you use fancy paper as money, by the way."

"You *robbed my neighbor*?" he hissed.

"I balanced the scales. That's not theft. It's justice. You like justice, don't you?"

"Did you do anything else?"

She giggled. "A thing or two."

"What else did you do?" he demanded.

"Guess."

Alan didn't have to think for long. There was one glaring windfall in recent history.

"Tell me you didn't steal that ticket for the charity dinner."

She rolled her eyes. "Please. I know you wanted it. And do you know *how* I know you wanted it? Because *I* know you wanted it. It takes a pretty intense desire for it to bleed through to someplace *I* can feel it."

"You can't just... Mr. Cox *assigns* those things. He's not going to just *forget* he didn't give it to me."

"You could have given it back, but you didn't. You wanted that assignment. I got it for you. You're welcome."

"But this was... it... he's going to accuse me of stealing it, and what am I going to say? 'No, I didn't steal it. My shadow did!' He'll laugh in my face."

"You should say, 'Here are all of the excellent pictures and videos I took. If you want more excellent pictures and videos, you should give *me* those jobs and not that awful woman of yours.' I don't like her. You know someone's due to be taken down a peg when they don't even have the good sense to stow their valuables properly. It should *not* have been so easy to pluck that ticket."

"I'm going to get fired..." Alan said.

"It's not a very good job anyway. I'll help you get a better one. That politician seemed like he had some good power. Why don't you do that?"

"I don't *want* to be a politician."

"But all the other—"

Her eyes opened wide and she thumped her cup down. Alan glared at her.

"All the other *what*?" he said.

"Never mind. You don't have to be a politician. We'll find something good for you."

"All the other *what*, Blot?"

"It doesn't matter."

"There are more of you, aren't there? There are more things like you floating around, and they are striving for positions of power just like you are."

"Don't say 'things like me.' We're not *things*. We're shades. And you just worry about you. You're going to be late for the assignment meeting if you don't finish getting ready."

Alan's mind and heart started to race. "Oh my god... If this is real, and you're not the only one..."

"Don't think too much about it, Alan," Blot said warily.

"This is an invasion."

"It isn't."

"A wave of people rushing into a place and trying to seize positions of power. What would you call that?"

"Not an invasion!"

"Why isn't this an invasion?"

Blot considered the question. "There are no... boats."

Alan cradled his head. "Oh god. What am I going to do..."

"We're not evil, Alan."

"Then what's it all about? Who are you? Why are you here?"

"It's... it's complicated, you know? You wouldn't understand."

"Being evasive isn't a sign of innocence, you know."

He brushed the mostly uneaten breakfast into a plastic container. Hopefully, tomorrow morning he wouldn't be grappling with an existential crisis and would have the time and appetite for it.

"It was the eclipse, wasn't it? All of the crimes afterward. The unexplained deaths. This is bad. This is bad."

"It isn't necessarily bad."

"How? How is an unexplained supernatural population insinuating themselves into the world not necessarily bad? What's the *good* version of this?"

She tapped her mug on the table for a moment. "Maybe you *are* crazy."

"Yeah. Great. Look at the bright side, you could be insane."

"I hate that phrase. What's so great about the bright side?"

Alan shakily dropped the plate into the sink.

"Look. You're nervous," Blot said. "I understand. This is strange. It's strange for me too."

He drummed his fingers on the counter and glanced at the clock. He had a few minutes to spare. "The eclipse..." He narrowed his eyes. "I never took a good hard look at the pictures of the eclipse."

Blot flitted up to stare at him from the countertop. "There's no reason to do that. You'll be late for work!"

He hurried to the bedroom and opened up his laptop. "I should have done this days ago. Things have been so crazy it slipped my mind. And if that's when you showed up..."

"Alan, really? What good will it do? You said it yourself: this could all be in your head."

He opened the time-lapse folder and scrolled to the apex of the eclipse. With the image zoomed to full screen, he leaned forward. Having only looked over the images in fleeting glances, he'd not noticed the little black streaks on the ground, stretching away from the tree in all directions. The angle was extreme, making details hard to pick out, but he could *just* determine that they were scrambling, faintly humanoid smears of black. He tapped his way through the pictures. There were more, and more. In some shots, the trunk of the tree was almost black with them. Hundreds of shades, pouring out like ants from a hill.

"Oh my god..." He slowly shut the screen of his laptop. "I'd better be crazy. Because I don't want to think about what this means otherwise."

"It doesn't mean anything, Alan. You just trust me and work with me and everything will be fine. You don't need to worry. You're my host. I'm not going to steer you wrong."

"You're fired," Mr. Cox shouted.

Alan had barely made it into the room. People were still milling about wondering what was taking him so long when the red-faced gossip magnate charged out of his office. Unsurprisingly, Marie-Anna was right beside him, righteous fury on her face.

"Did you think I wouldn't notice?" Cox said. "Just stealing the credentials right from another photographer? That is *not* how we do things in Cox Media."

"I didn't! Honest!" Alan said. "I just found it in my stack!"

This all felt alarmingly like he was a schoolboy getting a talking-to by the principal. When he'd been a child, he couldn't think of a worse fate. This was worse.

"He gave it to me, Alan," Marie-Anna snapped. "I'm his best society photographer. Who else would get it?"

"Get in my office. I want to have a word with you directly," Cox rumbled.

Alan walked past the gathered crowd of gawking photojournalists. Predictably, several snapped photos. A short trip down the hallway brought him to Cox's office. He'd never been inside it before, and frankly, it wasn't what he expected. Much of Cox Media was characterized by the popular new trend in floor plans. Lots of open spaces and glass walls. The sort of thing that is ostensibly supposed to support the free flow of ideas, but in reality is just to make sure no one gets enough privacy to be able to goof off. Cox's office wasn't one of those open-door policy fishbowls. It was rather small, rather dim, and tucked against the back wall. The windowless walls were covered with bulletin boards and plastered with printouts. The man didn't even snag the corner office for himself. It was the act of a man who was either very humble or trying to make sure no one else minded his business.

"The memory card, Alan," Cox fumed, flopping down into a leather office chair on the other side of a desk heaped with handwritten memos and index cards.

Alan handed over the card containing his coverage of the previous day.

"I can't believe you did this," Cox grumbled. "Do you know how hard it is to find someone who knows how to work one of those DSLRs the way you do?"

He jabbed the card into a reader and started dumping the files onto his PC. Full-resolution images popped up in his preview.

"Look at these. I barely have to tweak them! I swear, you're one of maybe five people I employ who knows what an f-stop is. If I grabbed one of those cameras from around the necks of the rabble in that bullpen, I guarantee you they'd have it set to automatic. It is going to be a pain in the ass to lose you."

It was the most absurd reprimand Alan could ever remember getting. In the months of working for Cox Media, he'd not heard a word of genuine praise from this man outside the empty motivational nonsense that he used to justify bad assignments. It took wrapping the compliments in fury over losing him to finally learn why he'd kept him in the freelance pool in the first place.

"Mr. Cox, it was a misunderstanding. I assure you. Maybe Jerry just handed out the wrong tag."

"Jerry never *had* the charity ticket. I gave it to Marie-Anna over... I gave it to Marie-Anna personally. You could only have gotten it from her."

The copy finished and he angrily tugged a desk drawer open to toss the memory card inside. He slammed it and locked it, then fetched a checkbook from another drawer. He tore a sheet from a legal pad and ran some figures.

"Five hundred photos. Seventy minutes of video..."

Alan sat uneasily in the poorly lit office. Out of the corner of his eye, he noticed his shadow sliding subtly out of alignment with the light.

"No," he hissed silently.

He had no clue what Blot had in mind, but in light of the current set of consequences for her bright ideas, and the potential nefarious motives for her arrival, he wasn't eager to have her roaming about his boss's office. She naturally didn't heed him, instead curling around behind the desk and out of view.

Mr. Cox scratched out a check. The sum was every bit as large as Alan had expected for a job of this caliber.

"There. I hope you choke on it. I had half a mind not to pay you at all, but we've got a contract, and I'm a man of my word." He cleared his throat. "And I already sold one of your shots for the above-the-fold coverage on the *Examiner*. But mark my words, this is the last time you'll ever work for Cox Media. I can't have someone working for me that I can't trust."

"Yes, sir. Sorry, sir."

Blot casually slid back into the proper position as Alan stood. He offered his hand for a shake. Cox glared at it.

"Get out," he demanded.

Alan nodded quietly and hurried out the door of the office. In the brighter light of the hallway, Blot snapped down and started oscillating up and down with each passing bank of fluorescents.

"What did you do?" Alan said.

"Nothing," she said as she swept past.

"I saw you roaming around in the office."

"Don't worry about it."

"You just got me fired. I have every right to worry about what you're doing!"

"You're going to make a scene," she said urgently.

He raised his eyes from his shadow to find he'd nearly marched right back into the assignment room while arguing with his own shadow. Marie-Anna was standing in the doorway of the room, arms crossed and a spark of spite in her expression. She made a show of zipping her purse tight and sliding it behind her as he walked past.

"We'll talk about this in the car," Alan murmured. "This isn't over."

A few minutes later, Alan was driving through town on his way back to his apartment. To an outside observer, he was having an angry conversation on his cell. In reality, he was in a heated disagreement with his shadow.

"What did I tell you? What did I tell you?!" he shouted. "You stole that ticket, and I felt the consequences."

"I'll make it up to you! I wouldn't have done it if I'd known you'd get caught."

"That's not even why you shouldn't have done it, Blot! You shouldn't have done it because it was *wrong*."

"Oh, for the love of darkness," she said. "Right and wrong don't mean a thing when the only people who care about them are good people."

"Exactly. So the solution is to get bad people to follow the rules!"

"Or get good people to ignore them and even the score."

"That's a terrible attitude!"

"You'll see. I know a thing or two about this. It's part of my education."

"Rule-breaking is part of your education?"

"Figuring out how to get done what needs to be done even when people are trying to stop you is part of my education. Rules are no good when the people making them are making them specifically to stop people like you."

"I just... stop distracting me. You were doing something in that office. Is this something that's going to be screwing me over even more?"

"Let's put it this way. He paid you a big pile of money just now, right?"

"Yes. And I'm lucky he did."

"And that's because those photos were worth a lot of money, right?"

"Yes."

"Maybe more than he actually paid you for them?" she proposed.

"Uh... I mean, yeah. Possibly. It's freelance. You sort of get whatever someone thinks they're worth. Someone else might've paid more. But it doesn't matter. I handed over all the copies to him."

Her shadowy hand slid over to his jacket pocket and slipped inside, then pulled out again.

"Are you *sure*?" she asked.

He took one hand from the wheel and jammed it in his pocket. Among the handful of change, a napkin, and a couple of sticks of gum was the very memory card he'd given Cox just minutes earlier.

"What... I don't even... how did you do that? The drawer was locked!"

"It doesn't take much of a gap for a shadow to slip through."

"But it takes a bigger gap for a memory card to slip through! And there wasn't anything in your hand just then."

"I've got my ways, Alan. Just be happy you've got those valuable pictures to sell."

"You don't... I can't believe you, Blot. I can't sell these again! I already sold them. He already has copies, they're already in his database. He's got a contract with my name on it that says I won't sell them. And even if he didn't, selling them would be a pretty scummy thing to do. And even if *that* wasn't wrong, *you just stole his property.*"

He turned, the sun causing her to sweep back behind him.

"You're making it very difficult to help build you up, Alan."

"Stop trying to help me!" he said. "Every time you do something for me, things get worse."

"I got you that big payday in your pocket."

"I... okay, fine. You did that. But it cost me the next couple of months of paydays I would have had if I'd stayed employed. So cool it. I've got to get home and figure out what to do from here."

"Can we get another coffee? The big one from the building tastes better than the one from your machine."

"No! I'm mad at you. And how do you even know what Vice Versa coffee tastes like? I haven't gotten any since I learned about... *were you drinking my coffee?*"

"I couldn't very well get it myself."

"You can't always get what you want, Blot! Just... stop talking to me. I'm done with you. I've got to get my whole life back on track because of you."

"It wasn't exactly on a great track when I found you."

He took a final turn toward his home. It was practically no surprise at all when he discovered a police car parked in front of the building.

"Oh... How much do you want to bet he's here about me? What do you think, Blot? Am I about to get arrested? Did I rob a bank and not notice it because of you?"

He heard her huff.

"Yeah, that's what I thought."

Alan stepped off the elevator and found a pair of police officers standing outside his apartment door. It was wide open. One of the officers was on his radio; the other was jotting down notes in a pad.

"Oh no... What happened?" Alan said.

"Crime scene, sir," said the taller of the two officers.

"This is my apartment," he said.

"Do you have some ID, sir?"

He dug into his pocket and fumbled for his wallet. "Here. There, see. That's my address."

The cop nodded. "There appears to have been a break-in, sir. Your neighbor—"

"Ms. Levitt," Alan surmised.

"Yes. She actually called us in on a noise complaint, but shortly afterward there was an alarm notification. Did you lock your door when you left, sir?"

"Of course. It's self-locking, actually. I know because I've been locked out a few times."

"There was no sign of forced entry. Either the robbers had a key, or they were able to pick the lock. Would you please step inside, sir?"

The police led him inside, where his apartment was a total disaster. Every drawer was dumped out. Every piece of furniture was pulled aside or overturned.

"Oh jeez..." he said, surveying the damage.

"I realize this may be difficult for you to determine, sir, but about how much would you say is missing?"

He looked around. Though the place was terribly disorderly, his eyes quickly came to rest on the big-ticket items. The flat-screen TV was pulled at an odd angle on its bracket, but intact and present. Likewise for the sound system. He had his good camera with him along with his laptop, but after wading through the mess of things, he found that his other camera and lenses, his backup hard drives, everything that seemed like it should appeal to a robber was still there.

"It uh... I mean, I won't really know until I clean up, but it doesn't look like anything major is missing."

"Jewelry? Watches perhaps?"

"I don't really have any stuff like that."

"Well. It seems like you lucked out. We've got some paperwork for you to fill out, if that is all right."

"Yeah, yeah, okay."

The other officer produced some forms and handed them over.

"Are you guys going to dust for prints or anything?"

The answer came from the doorway. "That won't be necessary."

Alan and the two officers turned to find a pair of individuals that were, in a word, striking. They were sharply dressed in flawless white suits that were just short of tuxedos in their elegance. White shirts with white ties showed behind the jackets. They even wore white sunglasses. Not just the glasses themselves, but the lenses were white. One of the visitors was a man, the other a woman. Both had the sort of long, lean, chiseled beauty in their faces and physique that suggested they could have just stepped off a catwalk during fashion week. Their beauty was of such a distinctive and similar sort that they could only be siblings. Alan could not conceive that that sort of elegance had happened in two different sets of genes. He couldn't take his eyes off them as they walked in.

"We are associates of these fine officers," said the beautiful man.

"Yes. We will take over the questioning, if you don't mind," said his partner.

The cops looked at one another, not so much puzzled as borderline disoriented.

"That's... yes. We'll just leave them to you, then," said the first officer to Alan.

"Be sure to turn those forms in at the station," instructed the other.

The police left, shutting the door behind them.

"You are Alan Fontaine, correct?" said the woman.

"Yes. And you are?" he said, holding out his hand for a shake.

The woman looked dispassionately at the offered hand, then looked back to him without accepting or returning the gesture.

"My name is Dina. This is my brother Gabriel."

"You're, um, investigators?" Alan said, wiping his hand on his pants in an attempt to play down the fact that he'd been left hanging.

"Would you mind clearing some seats, Mr. Fontaine?" Gabriel said.

"I'll do that, sure," he said.

He hastily cleared, straightened, and restored the cushions to the couch for his guests. He was halfway through before he even noticed he'd started. The act of hospitality was practically involuntary. When he was through, he paced over to the living room light and dimmed it. It was the only light in his house with a dimmer. Given the nature of his permanent guest, it seemed appropriate to keep the lights low.

Dina and Gabriel both took a seat and crossed their legs in unison. The cold detachment in their bearing, combined with the near-choreographed grace of their movements and their disarming beauty, put Alan in mind of old Robert Palmer videos.

He grabbed a chair from the kitchenette and turned it to face them. "So, do you have questions or..." Alan began.

"You indicated, if I heard correctly from the hall, that nothing appears to have been taken, correct?"

"Yeah. I mean, it doesn't seem like it. None of the big stuff."

Dina turned to her partner. "Gabriel?"

He reached into his pocket and withdrew a narrow silver pen and a long memo pad with unlined paper. He started scrawling something on the page while Dina continued to speak.

"You will of course answer us honestly when we ask you these questions."

"Of course," Alan said.

"Were you answering the police honestly when you made that claim, or were you attempting to hide something?"

"No, no. I mean, I could be wrong, but there's nothing obvious to me that was missing."

Gabriel finished with the pen and tore the page free. He presented it to Alan.

"Are you familiar with this, Mr. Fontaine?"

He took the page and found a remarkably faithful pen sketch of an ornate dagger. He could tell at a glance that it was the precise one he'd recovered from the would-be muggers. His eyebrows rose, and he looked to the end table he'd tossed it to. It wasn't there, nor anywhere on the floor nearby.

"That *is* missing," he said, standing. "Unless…"

"Sit down, Mr. Fontaine," Dina said.

He plopped down like a scolded puppy.

"We can assure you that the dagger is not present in this apartment. What we were concerned about was whether you were aware of its disappearance and trying to conceal it, or whether you were genuinely oblivious to its absence," she said.

"Both would be telling," Gabriel agreed.

"Well, no. I didn't think of it because I've only had it for a day."

"How did you acquire the weapon?" Dina asked.

"A couple of guys tried to rob me with it."

"You are certain they tried to rob you?" Gabriel asked.

"What else would they be trying to do?"

"Are you aware of the nature of the weapon?" Dina asked.

"Not really. I looked into it a little, but I didn't make much progress."

"Did your investigation turn up a group called The Dawn?" she asked.

"Actually, yes. You've heard of them?"

"We are familiar with them," said both of his guests in unison.

As the conversation rolled on, Alan found himself becoming uneasy. He couldn't quite put his finger on the cause, but every time he focused on one of the white-suited investigators, what his peripheral vision told him of the other didn't jive with what he knew to be true. Out of the corner of his eye, they looked different. Longer. Leaner. Considering how slender they were, the even more delicate build made them look almost inhuman. But each time he looked directly at them, there was no hint of what he thought he'd seen.

"Pay attention, Alan," Dina said.

He looked to her and focused upon the white lenses of her glasses.

"The Dawn is an organization with a near-religious obsession with certain supposed metaphysical phenomena."

"Like a cult?"

"The term is not precisely applicable, but it would not be out of place," Gabriel said.

"The knife that was briefly in your possession is of profound value to their cause. They are rare, and difficult to manufacture, so each one is extremely precious. It comes as no surprise that they would go to great lengths to retrieve it," Dina said.

"What's so important about the knife?" he asked.

"They believe it is capable of executing so-called 'shades.'"

Alan swallowed hard. His throat was getting dry, and his eyes burned a bit. He'd not blinked since she'd demanded his attention. "Shades," he said.

"It is a term they use for a supposed otherworldly threat. The details aren't important. Suffice it to say, if they had an interest in you, it may have been due to a belief that you were afflicted by one of these shades."

He swallowed again. "Uh-huh."

Dina removed her sunglasses, eyes shut beneath them, and fetched a kerchief from her pocket. When her gaze left his, he finally blinked, tears running down his cheeks as he looked away. His eyes fell on the floor. Blot had maneuvered herself away from the visitors as though *they* were the source of the light in the room. Her eyes were shut, and she did not even appear to be her diminutive self. She was a proper silhouette of Alan, indistinguishable from the real thing besides her curious behavior and a barely perceptible tremble.

"Alan?" Dina said.

He looked back to find she'd just replaced her sunglasses.

"Do you have any questions?" she asked.

"How did they find me? To take the knife back, I mean?"

"They have the means to keep track of their equipment," Gabriel said.

"Uh... Do I... should I be worried about these guys? The Dawn?"

"I wouldn't think so." She added with the faintest of chuckles, "Not unless you've got a shade."

Alan cleared his throat, but didn't speak.

Gabriel elaborated. "You will only cross paths with them if they believe you are afflicted, or if you have something they require. If we are correct and this theft was perpetrated by The Dawn, that they have not made a second attempt to confront you by now makes it a near certainty that you are not a target. In fact, if it took them a day to find the knife again, they must be stretched to the limit. So you will be safe unless you *make* yourself a target."

"What, uh... hypothetically, what would happen if I *was* a target?"

"They would find you and put that knife to use."

"And what would happen to me?"

"What do you think would happen to you?" Dina asked.

He coughed. "I think I would die."

"Interesting." She glanced to his feet. "Where would you get an idea like that?"

"I... ahem... just assumed. You know. Knives and all."

"Well, that is certainly the belief of The Dawn."

"They are killing people?"

"If you believe what they do, yes, they are most certainly killing people. But that requires a rather credulous point of view. They slice at shadows, not people. Or hadn't we mentioned that?"

"Are they evil?"

Dina and Gabriel laughed. A single, harmonious, humorless "Ha."

"That is a very unscientific question to ask, Alan," Dina said.

"Good and evil are a bit too subjective to be the topic of investigation," Gabriel added.

"*They* certainly see themselves as doing good work. They assign great evil to the shades, and view death to be preferable to subjugation."

"Subjugation?" Alan asked.

"We won't sit here and fill your head with their indoctrination, Alan," Gabriel said. "But suffice it to say, they believe control is the inevitable outcome of becoming afflicted by a shade."

"One could almost understand their view, if not for the presence of a cure," Dina said.

Alan raised his eyebrows. "Cure?"

"Certainly," she said. "It isn't a part of *their* doctrine."

"At least, not to our knowledge," Gabriel said.

"One would be hard-pressed to defend their actions as anything but evil if they *were* aware of the supposed cure for the supposed affliction."

"And what would that cure be?" Alan asked.

"Hardly relevant. The whole nonsense is laughable, isn't it?" Dina said.

He cleared his throat. "Laughable."

Gabriel and Dina stood simultaneously.

"I believe that will be all," Dina said.

"As we said, we do not believe you will have any further trouble with The Dawn," Gabriel said.

"And also as we've said, judging from recent activity from the group, they shouldn't have the time or person-power to spend on dead ends," Dina said.

"However, if you have a concern, keep this on your person."

Gabriel reached into his pocket. Alan expected something like a business card to follow. What came instead was a small silver bell. It looked like a decoration for a rich person's Christmas tree. He presented it to Alan.

"So what?" he said with a weak smile. "Should I ring it if I need help?"

Both of his guests looked at him mirthlessly.

"Goodbye, Alan," they said.

The pair let themselves out. When the door shut behind them, Alan practically collapsed into the chair. He'd not noticed it, but every muscle in his body had been tight as a guitar string while they were present. His throat burned, his eyes burned. It was like he'd been marching across the desert.

"They're gone, right. Tell me they're gone..." Blot said. Her voice was quivering, drenched in anxiety.

"Yeah." He coughed and hauled himself to his feet. "They're gone."

She snapped into the proper position for the light and resumed her true shape. Her hands, as far as he could tell from the silhouette, crossed her body in a hug, and she was rocking back and forth.

"I-I d-don't like them. I don't know what it is, I just—I don't—I didn't—I don't like them."

"They were just investigators," Alan said, shuffling into his disorderly kitchen to find a clean glass.

"They weren't 'just' anything," she said coldly. "They were... they were a lot."

"What were they then?" he said. "Because if they were something supernatural, they sure weren't here about *me*. They were here about *you*."

"We're the same thing now, Alan," she said, slipping up beside him. "And I don't know what they were. But they knew I was here. I could feel their eyes on me."

"But they didn't say anything... except..." He filled the glass from the tap. "They mentioned a cure."

"Which means they think I'm a disease. Why does everyone want to kill us?"

Alan guzzled the glass in one long series of gulps and took a grateful breath. "But is it true? Is there a cure? Is there a way to get me back to normal?"

Blot didn't answer. She appeared to be avoiding eye contact.

"Damn it, Blot. This is serious. This is my life!"

"It's my life too, Alan. If we separate, we both die."

"But I didn't always have you as my shadow. You must have been something before we were linked up."

"It's different. That's back... uh..."

"Blot, so far I've had a cult try to stab you off me, and I've had some ill-defined creatures who were 'a lot' come and question me. I'm not overly fond of you being my partner in all this, but it is what it is, so if we're *both* going to survive, we're going to have to work together. And that means you're going to have to come clean with me."

Now she locked her gaze with him. "You'd be willing to work with me?"

"As long as we're not going to have to do anything villainous."

"That's a matter of opinion."

He paced into his bedroom. "Then start answering questions and I'll form my opinion. Now, the cure?"

"I don't know. They don't teach us about cures. Or maybe they do, but..."

"Out with it," he said, returning the improvised shade to his lamp.

"I'm not very far along in my education. I've had a lot of training. But I haven't gotten good at much of it. I think that's why The Dawn didn't just kill me when they had the chance. I'm so weak they couldn't quite tell if I was even there. That's what that dangling thing was. It faces shades. I wasn't even powerful enough to stop it from wobbling."

"Okay." Alan nodded. "Okay, that's good news. And now they have their knife back, so they're probably not going to come after me again."

Blot looked away. "Well..."

"What?" Alan said, eyes narrowed and neck tight.

"I'm *going* to get more powerful. I wasted a lot of power to get here, and it's going to come back. I'm still not the *most* powerful, but I'm going to be someone they can find."

"Great..."

"That's why we've got to get you richer and more powerful, so you can defend yourself."

"They said something about control. That you would control me."

She shook her head. "Same as the cure, if there is one. I never learned how to do it."

"But it's true, then. Shades can control people."

"Only the best. And even then only the ones with the knack for it. For the rest of us, we'll never be able to make our host do something that it isn't in them to do. We can take a deep-down yearning and push it past the layers of inhibition, but we can't just seize control of your mind. Except for Stigma."

"Who is Stigma?"

"Stigma. The leader of this... the leader of what *you* would call an invasion. He might be able to just puppet his host." She fluttered her eyes and clutched her hands as if talking about a childhood idol. "He's the best of us. Already a legend."

Alan shut his eyes tight. "I've got to keep this small or I'm going to freak out... How much time do I have to get 'bodyguard rich' before a cult of assassins comes after me again?"

"I don't know. Not long. It depends on how fast I recover. Maybe weeks. Maybe less."

"I'm not going to get rich that quick."

"Not with *that* attitude. But you might not have to. I was trained on hiding myself from them. I'm sort of accidentally doing it now, weakened as I am. But there's a way to bury my extra strength so they can't detect it. If I can get that to work, we'll be safe. Or safer, at least."

"If you were taught to do it, why do you have to figure out how to do it?"

"Just because I know how it's done doesn't mean I know how to do it."

He tilted his head. "Want to try that one again?"

"Everything is different here. If you spent years reading all about swimming, but never dipped a toe in the water, you'd probably still flounder and sputter when someone tossed you in for the first time."

"I see. Theory versus practice."

"Right. You can't swim until you're actually in the water. This is all about adjusting to the way things are. It's a little different for every host. There's always a period of alignment. It's why things have to move slow. None of us are in top form right now."

"None of you... How many of you are there?"

"Lots. Lots and lots and lots. You saw in the pictures. We've been planning this for a while."

"Planning what? What is your plan?"

She turned away again. "You don't need to know that to plan how we're going to help each other."

"I need to know that if I'm going to know if we *should* be helping each other."

She huddled down a bit. "That's as far as I can go, Alan. I'm sorry. If you want to know more, ask something else."

He hissed an angry breath. "I'm good at putting together a picture out of little details. And I think I know where to start looking."

For what seemed like the hundredth time in the last few days, Alan was at his computer, clutching at straws and trying to find the truth. He kept the room dim enough for Blot to be able to watch over his shoulder. It was a courtesy, though for the life of him, he couldn't figure out why he was being hospitable to her.

"Please stop," she urged. "This is a waste of time. We should be figuring out how I can help get you on the road to fortune and power. You mentioned robbing a bank. We can probably—"

"Don't even think about it." He tapped his way through the photos and video from the memory card she'd stolen back from his boss. "There was someone from The Dawn outside the window... See, there?" He pointed to a frame of the video he'd taken. "Dangling the pendant thing. And it's rock solid. Way more solid than when *you* were the one he was looking for. So there was someone else like you at that party."

"So *what*?" Blot said.

"So I want to know who it was. It'll help me work out if you guys are doing something shady, and what it is."

"Something shady... There's another one of those phrases. You don't even try to *hide* how you feel about us."

"It's just a phrase," he said.

"There's a lot of them. I've been listening to the music and the radio along with you. Listening to what people say. Watching the TV with you. You're all about 'the forces of darkness' and 'dark times.' People who are smart are 'bright.' People who are stupid are 'dim.' If I'm doing something you don't like, I'm being 'shady.' You people clearly hate us, and you didn't even know who I was until recently. It's deep in you. You're afraid of the dark, and *we're* the dark. So you try to wipe us out. If you really cared, you'd be worried about what your people were planning on doing to *us*. We're the ones who are outnumbered and isolated."

"Don't read too much into it. There are other reasons for that kind of imagery than some instinctive hatred for supernatural creatures we've never heard of."

"Such as?"

He blew out a breath. "We can't see in the dark, so danger often lurks there. It blinds us. And nights are cold, days are warm. Sunlight makes things grow."

"Uh-huh..." Blot said dismissively.

Alan clicked through the photos. "The lighting in that place was too soft," he said. "There aren't enough strong shadows for me to be able to check if anyone's got a shade of their own. But most of the other people taking pictures were using their flash, so I should have some stuff in the videos."

"Just what are you hoping to find?" Blot asked. "If The Dawn know about whoever it is, then they're going to be on the run. Nothing to worry about."

"It's always better to know than to not know."

"Is it?" Blot asked. "You didn't know about shades and The Dawn and all that a few days ago. Now you do. Is it better now?"

"Blot, please, I've got a lot of video to go through. If you really want me to stop wasting my time and show some good faith, you could help me. Trust goes both ways. You've got to trust me."

"It *does* go both ways. How do I know that if I help you, you're not just going to go help kill one of my people, just because you don't like what they have planned?"

"Because I'm not a killer, Blot. You said it yourself: you can't make me do something it isn't 'in' me to do. That means you must be able to tell that sort of thing about your host."

"*Other* shades can. I already said, I don't have the hang of it."

"Well then do it like we do. Listen to my voice. Look in my eyes." He turned to her, looking into the white pools of her eyes. "I don't want *anyone* to die."

She recoiled a bit at the intense gaze. In truth, Alan felt it too. There was something about looking in someone's eyes. It caused a flutter of anxiety to ripple through him. Like the mere act of looking had bared something in his mind and soul. But like trust, the gaze went both ways. Despite being little more than blobs of white drifting in a jet-black silhouette, her eyes had something about them. A vulnerability. A fear. He saw someone lost, worried. Someone who was trapped in something over her head. He saw a lot of himself in those eyes.

Blot pulled back a bit and looked away. "You need to promise me. You need to promise me that you won't turn us in. That if I help you, I won't be stabbing my own people in the back. Don't make me a traitor, Alan."

"You need to promise *me* that your people aren't planning to kill any of ours. That you don't mean us harm."

She looked down. "I can't promise that. We've been given instruction on the things we need to do, but no one said anything about how we should do them. I don't want to hurt anyone. But shades are as different as humans are. Some of us might not worry so much about who gets hurt."

"Then a compromise. I promise I will do everything I can to make sure nothing bad happens to anyone. But if I see that someone means harm, I'll defend myself and my people."

Blot considered the offer. "I guess I can't ask for more than that." She narrowed her eyes in focus, and her insubstantial hand peeled away from the wall and extended toward him. It still had no detail, but as it moved and shifted toward him, it betrayed a dainty pudginess. "Deal."

He took her hand. The shadowy substance felt odd. Cool to the touch, but with the firm yield of real flesh. He gave a firm shake.

"Deal," he said.

Her hand slipped from his and pointed. "It was the man with that man," she said, before allowing her hand to flatten against the wall.

She'd indicated the silver-haired Senator Savage.

"There were a lot of men with him."

"Well it was one of them."

Alan brought up a list of thumbnails and video previews. He pointed to the various members of the senator's entourage. Blot shook her head each time.

"This guy? ... This one? ... How about..." He squinted at one of the previews for a video, then opened it up.

"Yes! Yes, that one there."

114

"The intern with the senator. I should have known. He was staring at me the whole time. He was probably actually staring at *you*."

Alan started to scrub through the footage. It took some time, but in another video he caught the senator and his men in the background looking over the charity paintings. For a single frame, a flash painted a normal shadow across the ground for the senator, and a similarly impish shadow for the intern.

"That's Dun. He was one of my instructors," she said.

"Why would he take the intern as his host and not the senator?"

"It isn't like we know exactly where to go or how to get there when we show up. And you felt what it was like to have no anchor in a place. We can travel pretty fast if we try, but there's only so much time before we have to choose someone. Most of us don't have more than a few hours to find someone. Some only have a few minutes."

"But he sure as heck found his way to someone close to a seat of power in a hurry," Alan said.

"It's what we're taught to do."

"This isn't good..."

"It's fine, don't worry about it," Blot said. "Like you said, he didn't get the senator. So you're fine."

"A supernatural entity has bound itself to someone with access to one of the most politically powerful people in the area. It could potentially be *terrible*." He leaned back in his seat. "We've got to do something."

CHAPTER 5

"This is a terrible mistake," Blot said. "You shouldn't be sticking your head up. That's a good way to get it cut off, and I need you with your head on. Being the shadow of a corpse won't do me much good."

"When in doubt, do the right thing," he said.

It had taken the better part of the day for Alan to work out who the intern was and where he lived. The pair was in Alan's car now, and his phone called out the next turn.

"I can't believe you found his address," Blot moped. "I thought for sure he would be harder to find than that."

"It turns out becoming an intern of a big campaign is something you brag about on social media."

"... The internet... I wish I'd had it to prepare. I'd have headed straight for this president of yours. I didn't even know you *had* a president. I was taught to look for lords and kings and things."

He took another turn. The setting sun allowed Blot to, with some difficulty, remain roughly cast upon the passenger's seat. Alan glanced at her briefly.

"We'll discuss that whole 'previous invasion' thing and your disappointment about not knowing our power structure later. Right now, I've got to figure out what I'm going to say to..." He glanced at the printout on the seat in front of her. "Lenny Castro."

"This isn't going to go well," Blot said. "Dun isn't going to be happy with me when he learns I told you as much as I did."

"Is Lenny going to know anything? Or am I about to inform him he's got a shadow like mine?"

"Dun will have persuaded him to help the cause. That's what he instructed me in."

"Manipulation?"

"He called it 'sculpting ambition.' I wasn't his best student..."

"Good for me, I guess."

"But Dun will definitely be teamed up with his host." She slouched a bit. "He has more to offer than I do..."

"What do you mean?"

"He'll have more power. He'll be able to do more things than I can. If he's got the sort of host who's hungry for power..."

"Right, right. I got it. But what sort of things?"

"I don't know, exactly. It depends on how compatible he is. He could be all the way to shape shifting, or just able to move and manipulate bigger objects from farther away than I can."

"... Shape shifting?"

"Yes. I can move a cup of coffee around by manipulating its shadow. To a degree, an object must do what its shadow does. Since *we* are *your* shadows, and we can change our own shapes, shades with the right training and enough power can change *your* shapes."

He blinked his eyes. "That's really unsettling."

"What are you planning to do?"

Alan shook off what she'd just said. "I'm going to try to talk sense into him. Into *them*, I guess."

"Talk sense into them? What does that even *mean*?"

"I'm going to find out their intentions and try to persuade them not to do anything rash."

"We trained to do this for *years*. You're not going to change his mind."

"I have to try. What if he's just trying to stay close to the senator until he can... I don't know, take him as a host instead."

"That's not the plan. Not the short-term one, anyway."

"How can you be sure?"

"Because he hasn't been here long enough to switch hosts yet. It's one of the most delicate and difficult things we can do. To be able to pull himself free from his current host and still have enough strength left to take a new one, he would have to be perfectly aligned with his host. That doesn't happen overnight."

"How long, then?"

"Unless it is a one-in-a-million perfect compatibility with his host, it'll be at least a few months. Probably more like a year. And then the same over again if he takes a new host. So there. The senator is safe. We can turn back."

"He's safe for a few months. Probably. That's not good enough for me."

"Be reasonable!" she urged. She motioned to pound her fist, but all she managed to do was briefly disturb the pages. "At least give us some time to get on our feet. Give me some time to learn this place better. Give me some time to *breathe* before you jump into the mess. I don't... I don't want to do this."

"Do what?"

"Whatever is about to happen! I don't want it. Either he'll try to do something to you, or he'll try to do something to me. Or you'll try to do something to him. It's going to be awful." She huffed. "It wasn't supposed to be this hard."

"Well I'm sorry I haven't been more helpful with the invasion," he said snidely. He glanced at her and caught a smoldering look in return. "Sorry. That was mean."

She growled. "See? That! It wasn't supposed to be like that!"

"What? I said I was sorry!"

"Exactly. You were supposed to be hostile. You were supposed to be this monster who would kill me as soon as look at me. And I was supposed to make myself valuable to you by appealing to your baser impulses. And if the things I was doing weren't in your best interest, I wasn't supposed to *care* because you were going to be a monster who deserved what you'd get. But you're not. You're *nice*."

"I... I haven't been the *best* host."

She pointed to the cupholder. "You bought me a cup of coffee on the way here! I didn't even ask!"

He replied sheepishly. "You said you liked the coffee from Vice Versa."

"You see! And you didn't even get one for yourself! They told me I should be prepared to face exorcists and angry mobs. No one warned me about cups of coffee and beautiful photographs and shades on the lights to make me more comfortable." She huffed and turned away. "You were supposed to be awful. I wasn't supposed to care about what happens to you."

"Blot, I'm... I'm touched."

"Well stop it. Be mad at me so I don't have to feel bad about being mad at you for not being mad at me."

He laughed. "You're a stupid smelly shadow and your hair looks funny."

She nodded sharply, the edge of her mouth curling into an unwilling grin. "That's better."

Alan pulled his car up to the address he'd tracked down. It was one of those not-quite apartment buildings. The place had likely started out as a duplex, but the stack of mailboxes suggested it was now home to a veritable army of roommates. He rang the doorbell, but there was no answer, so he headed back to his car.

"Are we leaving? We're leaving, right? He's not here, so we're leaving," Blot urged.

"It's still kind of early. Probably everyone's at work. We'll wait," he said, rolling the window up and turning on the radio.

He avoided the news. With the amount of disaster in his life so far, he really didn't need to hear about any other strange happenings right now.

He'd parked away from the nearby streetlight, and the fall sun had all but set, so Blot now had complete freedom in the car. She remained in the passenger seat with the shadow of the cup clutched in her grip. It hovered beside him, tipping back and producing a ghostly slurp and a fluttery murmur of anxiety every few seconds. The so-called snow-storm that had scared off so many of the planes hadn't met the meteorological expectations. The temperature had slid up above freezing soon after, and with the exception of the odd plowed-together mounds, there was little more than slush to worry about. That said, the mound of dirty ice not far behind his car reflected a touch more light inside.

"Are you okay now? Is the light okay?"

"It's fine."

"Have you calmed down a bit?"

"No. Now I'm thinking about those tall, skinny things in white."

"Right... You have no idea what they were?"

"No. But they knew what I was. That doesn't make sense."

"Why not? You said your people have been through here before. It stands to reason *someone* would remember you. The Dawn do."

"And I *know* about The Dawn. I didn't know that's what they were calling themselves, but I know who they are. I don't know what those things were. And they were *powerful*. The other shades should have let me know... Those things should have been part of my education."

"We're about to talk to your teacher. You can take it up with him... Him?"

"Him," she confirmed.

"You can take it up with him then."

"If we make it that far," she muttered. "Do you have that bell with you?"

"Yeah. You think I should ring it?"

"No! I think you should throw it away."

"They've really got you rattled."

"They were wrong. They weren't shades and they weren't humans. I *thought* those were the two things someone could *be*. Either the shadow or the thing that casts the shadow. What else could there be?"

"The light that casts the shadow," he said simply.

Blot considered this silently. "No," she decided.

"Why not?"

"Because you are shaped like a person. And the shadow you cast is shaped like a person. That makes sense. But you never have *light* shaped like a person."

"I sort of meant it like a metaphor."

"This isn't a metaphor. This is reality." She gazed out the window. Now and again her mouth would open, then shut again without forming any words.

"What's on your mind?" he asked.

She looked to him, measuring him with her gaze, then set the cup down in the cupholder. "What would you do, if not for what *I* was supposed to do?"

He cocked his head. "I don't follow."

"We're, you and me, we're in this together. And that's my fault. And I have this thing I'm supposed to do. But if I didn't, and we were still in this together, what would you do?"

"I'm doing it," he said. "I'd try to stop the others, and—"

She shook her head. "Without the others, too. If it were just you and me, in this situation, with nothing else to worry about."

"Oh. I don't know. What would you do?"

She released a long breath from her nose. "I'd see more. Those pho-tographs. I'd see some of them. The places where they were. Or new places."

"Yeah," he said with a grin. "I guess that's what I'd do if things were reversed. A whole new world to see."

She shook her head. "No. If things were reversed, if you were where I came from, you wouldn't like it. It's just black and white. Brightness and dark. The sky is white. The stars are black. No color. Not really. It's not a nice place. This place is more interesting."

"Still. I'd like to see it. There must be some good stuff back home. Your family..."

She shook her head again. "No family. Not anymore. The last family I had was my grandmother. That's why I started getting training for this. Most of us who come over here are orphans."

"I'm so sorry. What happened to your family?"

"Like I said. It's not a nice place."

"It'll feel better if you talk about it."

She looked away. "It'll feel better if I forget about it."

"I..." He glanced up. A car pulled into a spot in front of the building, and the intern stepped out. He glanced about, a hunted look on his face, and hurried into the house.

"This is it," Alan said.

"You can still change your mind. You can still drive away."

"No. I've got to find out what he's planning. And if it's bad, I've got to try to stop him. It's the right thing to do."

"Lots of people get killed doing the right thing," Blot sulked.

Alan approached the front door and leaned on the bell. As near as he could figure, it wasn't doing anything. He tried to look through the window, but the inside of the house was extremely dim. As far as he was concerned, that was a good sign. Maybe it meant that the intern and his shade had a similar rapport and they'd be reasonable.

After getting sick of waiting, he knocked on the door. Some thumping and cursing ended with the door swinging open a crack, limited by a chain. A clearly concerned and confused eye appeared in the crack of the door and glanced up and down.

"We don't want any," he said.

"Wait!" Alan said, before the door could slam. "I just wanted to talk to you about—"

Before he could launch into what would no doubt sound like a very strange bit of religious proselytizing, the eye glanced down at his shadow.

"Another one?" he muttered under his breath.

A white eye loomed up behind him, then a harsh voice grumbled something. The door slammed shut, the chain rattled, and then the door opened fully.

"Inside. Get inside," hissed the man, pulling Alan into the darkened front room.

He hastily slammed the door shut and fastened the locks. Alan glanced around. Something unusual was clearly going on here. The place was largely empty, and the way the remaining furniture stood at odd angles and furniture-shaped depressions marred the carpet made it clear that everything else had been removed recently and hastily. The windows were covered, but in a far more "hide from the world" sort of way. Those windows with thick enough blinds and drapes merely had them closed. Others had everything from blankets to bath towels taped or tacked over them.

"Lenny Castro?" Alan said, turning back to him.

The young man was peeking through the small marbled-glass window in the door as though Alan may have been followed.

"Yeah, yeah, that's me." He glanced over his shoulder. "You're the... uh... you're from the charity thing, right? The festival thing?"

"That's right."

"Yeah. I thought I saw..." He vaguely gestured to Blot. "That."

His shadow slid up the wall beside Alan and looked him over. Blot sheepishly slid up beside it. In silhouette, it was difficult to make out the position she had assumed, but her hands were held in a peculiar and unnatural way, palms together but inverted, like she was trying to shake her own hands. She lowered her head once, then straightened up. She was half a head shorter than Dun, and while she was fairly plump in her physique, Dun was broad-shouldered and jagged-eared.

"Blot, I am frankly astonished you survived," said Dun.

His voice was different from hers. She, at least, could have sounded human. Dun's voice reverberated with a windy echo. Alan wondered if it was how he truly sounded, or simply how a shade sounded to someone who was not its host.

"He wasn't followed, Dun," Lenny said, trotting back.

In the dim light, Alan had trouble making out the young intern, but he looked ragged, like he hadn't slept.

"Impressive..." Dun leaned low, inspecting her more closely. "No. I suppose not. You've barely got the strength to turn a pendant."

"Yes, Dun. But I am recovering nicely, I swear!"

"So, what is this one?" Dun asked, gesturing at Alan.

Alan held out his hand. "I'm Alan Fontaine. I'm a photographer."

Dun turned to him and gave him a look of empty confusion, as though a dog had tried to answer the question.

"I am discussing this with my associate," he said, gesturing dismissively. "Talk to the boy."

Dun turned back to Blot and resumed his discussion. Alan turned to Lenny.

"If you need a place to crash, Dun had me buy out the other guys. Next door, too. This place is all mine now." Lenny leaned forward conspiratorially. "Did yours do the 'reach into the ATM' thing?"

"No."

"They can just empty them out! Takes like two seconds and then you've got a couple thousand dollars in cash. Anyway. Uh, you can stay here. He's got the place... what's the word... warded! Yeah. So The Dawn can't find the place..."

"That is not what I asked you!" Dun barked at Blot.

Lenny flinched at the outburst. Everything about his body language made him seem like a terrified Chihuahua with an abusive owner.

"He is very capable. We have established an... er... our relationship is collaborative," Blot said.

Dun scratched his head. "A photographer... It can be made to work. Lenny, Senator Savage can use a photographer, correct?"

"Oh, sure. Yeah. The campaign is lousy with photographers. Another one on the payroll won't be questioned. You just have to get me into the computer again."

"You hear that, Alan!" Blot said. "You can be a photographer for a senator! That's pretty good, right? That's not bad! Let's do that."

"Dun, listen. We need to talk. I need to know what you've got planned."

He glared at Alan. "You'll know what I have planned when I decide you have a part in it."

"I'm afraid that is unacceptable," Alan said.

"Hey, buddy. You're going to want to go easy. Once you've seen what these things can do..." Lenny warned.

"I don't want anyone to get hurt," Alan said.

Dun turned to Blot. "Get him under control," he warned.

"Alan, please. I—"

"'Please'!" Dun proclaimed. "Blot, did I tell you to *plead*? Get him under control, or I will consider you a liability."

Blot turned and took a deep breath. When she spoke, her voice had an eerie depth that *almost* concealed the quiver of anxiety.

"Alan Fontaine you will shut your mouth and await your orders as we have discuss—*as I have commanded!*"

There wasn't an ounce of real power behind the command, aside from the theatric delivery, but it was clear what was on the line, so Alan did his best to appear genuinely cowed.

"Right, Blot. I am sorry. I spoke out of turn," he said.

She gave a firm nod. "And *don't* do it again."

Blot and Dun continued their discussion. Alan turned back to Lenny.

"Don't pull that crap again, man," Lenny said. "We've got a good thing going here. It's like a guardian angel who doesn't care about laws."

"But they aren't exactly doing it out of the kindness of their own hearts, are they?"

"Look, you do what they say, they drag you right up the ladder. It's not like it's *that* bad. I just have to linger and listen, you know? Check some computers. Get some—"

"Silence! Your role is none of his concern!" Dun said.

"Right! Sorry, sorry," Lenny said.

Dun and Blot continued their discussion. Alan tried to listen, but when Dun was not addressing him directly, the shade's voice steadily declined until he was nearly silent. Since he wasn't actually a physical being, Alan supposed he didn't need to be heard if he didn't choose to be heard. That meant that all he could hear were Blot's occasional assertions and agreements, and barely those.

"Hey, man. You want a beer or something? Whenever Dun gets to talking to one of his own, it always takes a while."

"So he is in contact with—"

"Uh-uh-uh! You want to get him pissed at us again? Less talking, more beer."

Alan nursed a beer and watched out of the corner of his eye as the shadows talked. He really wasn't much of a drinker, and now was no time for him to have his thinking clouded, so he took it easy. Lenny was notably less moderate in his intake.

"It was a little hard to believe, you know?" the intern said, tossing aside his second can in five minutes and cracking another. "I had this dream where this guy came in. Usually, you know how a dream sort of flows and everything feels natural no matter how unnatural it is? Not this time. He showed up and the brakes just went on. One minute I'm dreaming I can't find my shoes and a cruise ship is about to leave; the next this guy is here, suit and tie, steely glint in his eye. Sort of like that *Twilight Zone* guy. He starts talking to me like my therapist, trying to work out what I want out of life and what I'd be willing to do to get it. He talks about how even the *littlest* advantage over everyone else is all it would take to be king of the mountain."

He drained half the beer in one guzzling swig, then wiped his mouth and continued. "I woke up, and the guy was gone, but the voice wasn't. And there he was, plastered against the wall by the sun. Glaring at me. A few hours later..." He tugged open a drawer to reveal a stack of loose twenties. "Things were lookin' up! What's yours done for you?"

"She's why I got the job working that charity thing you saw me at," Alan said.

"There, you see!"

"She's also the reason I got fired from that job."

"Oh... Well, I mean, maybe you got a clunker, but you'll be working for the senator by tomorrow. It'll be good to have another 'host' around. This guy can get a little spooky just hanging around in a dark room with him." He nudged Alan. "If you're lucky, we'll get you a better job after that, because pretty soon the *real* job to be after will be—"

"We're through here," Dun said. "I have heard what I need to hear."

"Great!" Lenny slapped Alan on the back. "Welcome to the team!"

"There is just one thing that remains to be done." Dun beckoned with his finger, eyes locked on Alan. "Approach."

Alan stepped up to the wall such that Blot was on one side of him and Dun was on the other. His own shadow looked a bit more relaxed. The conversation must have gone well enough that she wasn't fearful of discovery anymore.

"You were insubordinate," Dun said simply. "That is unacceptable."

"Again, I am sorry. I spoke out of turn."

"Apologies are meaningless. You learn from your mistakes only when they have consequences." He turned to Blot. "Discipline him."

Her eyes widened a bit. "I... I maintain control through other methods."

He leaned closer to her. "Your methods have clearly been ineffective. I am your instructor. You will do as I instructed."

"I... cannot yet do as you instructed. I have not recovered sufficiently."

"What's this about?" Alan asked.

Dun surveyed Blot critically, but he nodded.

"Very well. Watch closely. The sooner you can achieve this, the more obedience you can expect."

The instructor's hand shot from the wall. It twisted and curled, becoming more like the jagged shadow cast by a gnarled tree branch. The twisted hand curled over his head and clutched it tight. He tried to pull away, but the grip was punishing. His hands wrapped around the fingers and he tugged fruitlessly at them. They felt like bone and sinew. The claws at the tips dug like needles into his head. The pain was exquisite. Alan couldn't even scream. His voice caught in his throat as the pain penetrated deeper and deeper.

"H-he is my host! I will discipline him myself!" Blot urged.

"Silence. A proper lesson leaves scars. A proper lesson will be remembered," Dun hissed.

"S-stop!" Blot insisted. "I need him alive and well!"

"I will not cripple him. But he must suffer..."

Alan's vision was beginning to fade as the pain grew so much deeper than anything he'd ever felt before. There was no way this was the cruelly sharp claws alone. There was something else at work. Some sort of venom, or perhaps some sort of curse. He felt his legs weakening beneath him.

"Don't hurt him!" Blot shrieked.

A sickening crack rang out and the pain lifted away. Alan crumbled to the ground. As the deep purple and blue clouds blotting out his vision cleared, he saw a fearsome sight. Blot and Dun were gone. Or, at least, the *shadows* were gone. Now, black forms rose up from the ground. They were twisted, stretched. Gangling arms tipped in long, crooked fingers and rapier claws clutched and sheared at the air. Their mouths were like holes torn in the terrifying, featureless faces, the same brilliant white as the eyes that waved and flickered like flame. One of them was so large its head nearly scraped the ceiling. The other was barely larger than Alan, and it flickered and juddered in place, as though constantly threatening to snap back into two dimensions. Alan didn't need to be told which was Blot.

"Oh god, oh god, oh god," Lenny yammered, curling up in the corner. "Not this. Not again."

"If you will not use your host properly..." seethed Dun in a far more monstrous version of Dun's voice. "Then you are a liability. You must both be destroyed."

Dun slashed at Alan. He scrambled back. The claw fell just short, gouging into the carpet and peeling it back.

Blot charged toward Dun. She slashed at his face. The blow was glancing, but enough to force a minor retreat. Alan's now-monstrous shadow turned to him. She pulled him from the ground and put him on his feet. It was a struggle to do even that. Her twisted, terrifying form was easing closer to her less frightening self with each passing moment.

"Alan, run!" she urged.

Dun recovered and smashed into her. Both dark forms crashed into a wall. Plaster shattered. Alan, once again heeding the call to flee, rushed past them as they tangled.

"Stop him!" demanded Dun.

Alan reached the door. In his haste, he tried to haul it open without first undoing the deadbolt and chain. He attempted to force the sounds of supernatural combat from his mind and focus on the locks. An impact from the side knocked him painfully into the wall beside the door.

Lenny had tackled him.

"I'm not letting you screw this up for me!" he growled, then heaved Alan to the floor of the main room and straddled him. "At least you'll give me a chance to earn some points with Dun..." he said with demented glee.

Lenny balled up his fists and started pummeling. It was a manic, flailing attack. Fists peppered Alan's face with blows. Having so carefully run from every fight that had come along, Alan lacked even schoolyard combat skills. All he could do was struggle and try to throw the smaller man off.

He gathered himself for the best shove he could manage. The weight atop him vanished. Lenny launched backward and hung in the air for a moment before Alan realized there was a claw wrapped around him. Blot had snatched him up. She was nearly as large as Dun had been, but shuddering and skewing like a poorly tuned TV from a black-and-white film. She heaved with all of her might, lofting Lenny across the room. He struck a window. It shattered and the improvised blackout shade fell away.

Light from the streetlight poured in. Instantly, both Blot and Dun snapped against the far wall, pinned there by the brightness. She'd entirely lost her monstrous form, reverting to her more impish silhouette. The same could not be said of Dun. He towered over her form now, eyes smoldering points of fury. Even in the bright light, he maintained a measure of his physicality. Lashing claws splintered the floorboards.

"I... I can't..." Blot panted.

Alan rolled out of the pool of light, freeing Blot.

"You've got to get us out of here," she urged.

He scrambled to his feet and dashed for the door.

"Down!" she suddenly screeched.

Alan felt something snag his foot and he sprawled forward. A heartbeat later a half-empty bookshelf launched across the room, shattering against the door. He rolled to his back and scrambled away as Dun fought to tear himself entirely away from the wall. Lenny was slowly recovering, but he was still in the pool of light. Dun, for all his clear strength, couldn't quite free himself until Lenny could crawl into the darkness. That wouldn't take more than a few more seconds.

Alan looked desperately about. The door was blocked by debris, and any attempt to dash for a window would put him in range of the slashing claws as he tried to reach it. This was it. He was going to die.

"Hold your breath," Blot said wearily.

Alan did so, heaving a deep, terrified breath just as Lenny moved far enough toward the wall for Dun to drag him the rest of the way out of the light. Two black arms reached up on either side of Alan and hugged him under his arms. He shut his eyes. The arms pulled tight.

A ripple of icy cold rose up around Alan. He felt like he'd broken through the surface of a frozen lake and was now floundering in the water beneath. It was chilling, but the sensation went so much deeper than his flesh. It reached his very core. He opened his eyes, but what they showed him didn't make sense. The world before him slid about like something projected on a massive screen. The colors were wrong, drained to gray. And the lines were wrong. Shapes didn't recede in the distance as perspective would dictate. They retained a geometric straightness. Things flickered and flashed in front of his vision. He looked up to see the debris and door sliding down toward him like they were falling from above. They flitted past his face, near enough that he expected them to scrape at his nose, but instead he glided smoothly beneath them and into the street.

When the light of the streetlight hit him, it felt like gale-force wind, washing both him and Blot across the ground to the edge of its light. His chest started to heave for air as he felt their path arch up and slide across the hood of his car. They passed through the glass of the windshield like it was mist. Finally, he felt the grip on his chest loosen and the color and warmth of the world rushed back in.

"What?! What just... where are we?" Alan gasped, trying to make sense of the torrent of sensations. He was in the seat of his car. The door was still locked. Ahead, the door of Lenny's home was still shut. "Did you just... was I just a shadow?" he said.

The door to the building flew open. Lenny staggered out into the light. "Just drive!" Blot cried.

He fumbled for his keys and jabbed them into the ignition. Lenny's limping turned into a terrified sprint toward Alan's car. One could only imagine the threats Dun was shouting in his ear. The closer he got, the more three-dimensional his monstrous shadow became, lurching up out of the street and beginning to loom over him.

Alan got the car started and switched on the high beams. The light hit Dun like a freight train, smashing him backward and flattening him to the ground.

"Run him down!" Blot commanded.

Tires squealed as he slammed his foot on the accelerator, but he pulled the wheel hard to avoid hitting Lenny. A horrid metallic screech rang out as they sped past the thrashing shadow and went squealing into the night.

Halfway across town, Alan slid into the darkened corner booth of a diner. His eyes were wide and twitching.

"Can I get you anything?" a waitress asked.

Alan jumped at the sound of her voice. He looked up. "Uh... just. Let me have two coffees, please."

"You expecting someone else?" she asked.

"No. Two coffees please. Thank you," Alan said.

"Coming right up."

She paced away. Blot slowly slid up beside him. Though the peculiarities of her shadowy form couldn't be seen by anyone without a shade of their own, she still huddled close, her form practically nestled under Alan's arm while he fought to get his heart to stop pounding.

He waited until the two cups were poured before he spoke. There was no way he was going to avoid looking like a lunatic right now. He wasn't entirely certain he *wasn't* a lunatic. But it was still probably a good idea to hold off on talking out loud to himself until he could be assured of at least a few minutes free of waitress visits.

Alan raised the coffee to his lips and took a sip. He tried to focus on the heat of it rolling down his throat. It curled through a body that still felt horribly cold.

"I think we have some new things to discuss, Blot," he said.

"I warned you," she said quietly.

She tried to lift her cup, but it just rattled weakly at the table. She was clearly spent from the effort of the battle and escape. He stuck a stirrer into her coffee cup in lieu of a straw. She slid over to its shadow on the wall and slurped gratefully at the hot beverage.

"We'll set aside the less-than-successful attempt at defusing the situation," Alan said. "It seems like you can do a hell of a lot more than I thought you could."

"I can do a hell of a lot more than *I* thought I could do. The strength is coming back faster than I expected."

"Let's make a list, shall we? You can turn into a twisted inky monster."

"Combat form," she said.

"Right. That was new."

"It's not easy. I don't like it. I was *really* bad at that when I was training."

"You seemed pretty good at it to me. And then there was the... uh... hug."

"I wasn't sure that would work."

"Oh. Great. Glad I could help you with a little experiment. Care to go through what exactly happened?"

"I pulled you into the shadows. It's the same as when I stole the memory card, and the opposite as when I pull out of the shadows to have substance. It's easy with simple, small things. A whole, living, breathing being—much harder."

"But you're my *shadow*. I'm casting you. If you pull *both* of us into the shadows, who is casting *me*?"

"No one. We're unanchored."

"Like when you peeled away from me."

"Yes."

"Like you said would kill you—us—if it went on for too long."

"Yes."

"So we almost died."

"No. We were doing a thing that would have killed us if I did it too long."

"Which is different how, exactly?"

"Proximity to death," she said. "We would have almost died if I'd done it for, I don't know. Five, ten more seconds."

"Glad that I was five seconds further from death than I thought."

"We were closer to death *before* I hugged you. Dun would have killed you, and that would have killed me. And that was your fault, by the way."

"Right. Yes. True. I'll cop to that."

They both sat silently, sipping their coffees.

"Thank you," he said.

"Don't thank me," she said. "I didn't really do it for you. I did it for us. Which means I did it for me."

Alan shook his head. "Doesn't change the fact that you saved my life."

Blot nodded. "You're welcome, then."

"Seems like you and I have a much better partnership than Lenny and Dun."

"Technically, based on what I was taught, he's got the better host." She sipped her coffee. "But I'm starting to think maybe I didn't get the best education."

"So... how long before this all explodes in my face? There was just a huge rumble. The cops are going to have to get involved."

Blot shook her head. "Dun won't want human authorities involved. He'll try to deal with it himself. And he won't do *that* if it means taking time away from the mission or exposing himself to the threat of The Dawn."

"The mission."

She sighed. "You want me to tell you what I know."

"At this point, we're both probably marked as enemies of the cause."

"Probably the only way we're going to survive is if we stop the plan or know how to get out of the way," she said.

"That's what I was thinking."

She looked to him. "That's not supposed to matter to me, you know. I'm supposed to put the mission ahead of my own life. It's the only important thing. It's war."

"So it *is* an invasion."

"It's a preemptive strike. That's what they call it, anyway. They teach us that you people want to destroy darkness. And they teach us that if you *know* about us, you'll want to destroy us. So to survive, we have to find a way to stop you. That means—"

"Wiping us out first?"

"No!" Blot said. "We're not evil. That's not the plan. That was never the plan." She turned her head away. "We're supposed to control you. We're supposed to acquire leadership roles."

"You're trying to take over the world."

"It sounds bad when you say it like that," she said. "But it's not *wrong* I guess. There's lots of us. We spread out from where we arrived as much as we could. We're supposed to latch on to positions of power and, when we can, take them as hosts."

"And then what? Just be in control forever?"

"I was fodder for this thing. My training didn't include 'and then what.' My training stopped at 'until you die or get further orders.'"

"Sounds like a hell of a life."

"It seemed a lot more heroic before I met you."

"And this is happening all around the country?"

"That's the idea. This is the most sensitive part of the plan. We're all weak. We will be for a few months."

"That thing that tried to crack my skull like an egg and threw me against a wall was *weak*?"

"Relatively." She struggled to slide her coffee a little closer. "Right now, The Dawn is wiping us out wholesale. We're taught to assume that if we make it to the next full moon, we're among the one in ten who lived. I really don't think it'll be that many. You're much better with bright light than you ever were before."

Alan felt a darkness in the pit of his stomach. Even knowing their plan, and how bad they could be, his empathy squeezed his heart at the thought of so many of them dying, especially if most of them were orphans forced into it as cannon fodder. Then another thought came to mind.

"Wait... All of the ones that are still alive have hosts."

"Yes."

"And when The Dawn takes them out, the hosts die too."

"Yes they will."

"So The Dawn are mass murderers twice over." His brain ticked a few steps further along in the plan. "And if things keep going the way they're going, if we get to the point that you guys start getting new hosts, all of your original hosts will die, all of the new hosts will be powerful people, and The Dawn will be assassinating *them*."

"Sounds right."

"Who are the good guys in all this?"

"Since when does there have to be good guys? Nature doesn't have good guys and bad guys. It has predators and prey. And most things are both at the same time."

He sipped his coffee. "I'm not feeling very predatory."

"What's that tell you?" she said sulkily.

They both stared into the middle distance. The waitress came to freshen their cups.

"... Do they just come and give you more coffee without asking? Is that just what they *do* here?" Blot asked.

He looked to her, grinning a bit. "Yeah. That's a diner thing."

She smiled distantly. "I like it here. ... Even if the coffee isn't as good as Vice Versa."

"So what are we going to do now?" he asked.

"I'd like to sit here awhile longer. Maybe pretend like we're not at the middle of a storm of things trying to kill us..."

"I like that plan."

Another peaceful moment passed.

"You don't eat, but you drink, right?"

"I don't *have* to eat or drink. But I can do both."

"Have you ever had a milkshake?"

"I'm not even sure what one is."

Alan flagged down the waitress. When she stepped up, he squinted at her name tag.

"Honey?" he said. "Your name is Honey?"

"That's what the tag says," she said with a grin.

"Well, Honey, I'm Alan. And I'm curious, do you happen to have mocha ice cream?"

"We sure do."

"Two mocha milkshakes, please," he said.

"Two... One at a time or both together?"

"Together."

"And no one's meeting you?"

"Nope."

She shrugged. "Coming right up." The waitress paced off.

"After this, we've got some serious talking ahead of us. Did Dun say anything to you about what he had in store?"

Blot slumped. "No. Mostly he was just interested in what I could tell *him*. Which wasn't much. But I know that it has to do with two politicians."

"Two? So Senator Savage and Commissioner Magnuson are both involved."

"Uh... No. One of them is involved and the other isn't. And I think the goal is to make the one who's involved win."

"We already know Savage didn't have a shade. So that means..."

"Alan?"

"Yeah?"

"Coffee and milkshake first, please."

"Yeah. Good thinking."

CHAPTER 6

Alan sat back down in his car and shoved some snack wrappers out of the way. A cold rain tapped across the windshield. Their plotting and planning had taken more than a day. This had given them both a bit of time to recover, though you'd never know it by looking at Alan. His lumps were bruises, and his gouges were scabs. Overall, he looked like someone who had the bad habit of losing fights, which was a fairly accurate depiction of his existence these days.

"Are you sure you know what you are doing?" Blot asked, squinting into the blurry distance. "I can't see a thing."

"Trust me, this has been an unpleasant part of my job for the last couple of months. I've gotten good at it."

He'd parked several blocks away from Lenny's house. It was only barely visible in the distance, hidden even more effectively by the steady rain. But he'd mounted his camera, hooked it up to a long-life battery, and trained it on the doorway.

"If you want a photo of someone elusive, it's all about managing the distance. Far enough that the security doesn't know you're watching, but close enough that you can keep the shot in frame."

"And people pay good money for blurry pictures of famous people from far away?" Blot asked.

He gave her a hard look. "My photos are not blurry. But yeah. The harder it is to get a picture, the more people will pay for it."

"Not more beautiful, or more meaningful. Just harder to get?"

"Those things too, but an elusive subject tends to get the highest price."

"You people are weird."

"No argument from me. What do you people do, art-wise? It sounds like you don't have the technology we have."

"If we do, I've never seen it. But... art... I don't know. Art isn't a thing you capture, back home. It's something you experience. You go to the place where beauty is and just... be a part of it."

"Sounds nice."

"Yeah. If you can get to those places." She leaned aside and huffed. "I guess it's the same then. Rare and elusive is the most valuable."

"You'd said that if you had it your way, you'd travel. See the sights. That makes even more sense now."

"You remember that?"

"Sure. My mother taught me to be a good listener."

"My grandmother taught me to make soup and keep my head down. That's it."

"Is that what you did back home? Were you a cook?"

She glanced at him. "You're being nice again, Alan."

"Ideally, I never stopped. But I could call you smelly again if you want."

"I don't think a host and a shade are supposed to be friends. I've certainly never heard of it."

"Maybe there'd be a lot more of this if things didn't start off so sh... sneaky."

"You were going to say 'shady,' weren't you?"

"Old habits die hard."

"Same here. I keep feeling like I should be working toward the mission instead of..."

"Instead of what?"

She looked to him. "How do you think this is going to turn out, Alan? I can't help you without hurting my own people. And I can't help my own people without hurting *your* people. Someone has to get hurt. And it would have been worlds easier if I didn't mind it being you."

"The world gets a lot better when we start caring about what happens to other people, Blot."

"Either that or the people who care a lot have miserable lives spent feeling anxious over strangers while the people who don't care stomp all over everything."

"Well aren't *you* a little ray of sunsh... Boy, we *do* play the 'light is good, dark is bad' card a lot, don't we?" He glanced at the camera's preview screen. "Okay, he's on the move."

"How do we know he's going off to do no good?" she asked. "Couldn't he just be going to work?"

"I studied the senator's schedule. Near as I can figure, there's nothing official going down today. That *should* mean nothing that requires the intern. Considering it was implied that Dun is powerful enough to attract The Dawn, I can't imagine he'd go anywhere outside without protection unless he had to. So whatever he's off to do is probably important to Dun."

"That makes sense."

145

Alan watched as the perpetually rattled Lenny slipped into his car. Alan started the engine.

"Time for another paparazzi staple. Trailing the limo..."

Being a photographer for the sort of stuff Cox cared about meant Alan had to develop some less-than-noble skills. Keeping tabs on Lenny and Dun put those skills to the test. Philadelphia wasn't the most pleasant city to navigate, and doing so while trying to maintain a reasonable distance and a low profile was harder still.

After an hour of roundabout driving and some false positives later, Lenny pulled into the parking lot of a warehouse. Both the lot and the warehouse looked to be largely deserted, so Alan couldn't pull the same "park far away and keep an eye on it" stunt. If he were near enough to see what was happening here, he would be near enough to raise suspicions.

That was just as well. This particular meeting fairly screamed "gathering of the secret cabal." If he was going to learn something useful, it was going to be here.

He drove past and managed to snap some barely passable pictures of what few other cars were in the parking lot. He also spotted and clicked subtle shots of a half-dozen heavily built gentlemen. Most were not-so-subtly letting their hands hover at belt level outside trench coats, rather transparently telegraphing the concealed weapons within. When he was satisfied he'd done all he could do without turning any heads, he found his way to an out-of-the-way location to stop the car.

"What now?" Blot asked.

"I want to know what's going on inside," Alan said.

"That makes sense, but wanting to do something and actually doing it are a long way apart."

"Ideally, I'd want video. And audio. What I *need* to do is get a camera in there. Any way you can help, maybe?"

"Such as?"

"I don't know. You showed off a bunch of useful powers I didn't know about yesterday. I thought maybe you'd have a deus ex machina up your sleeve."

"You've seen pretty much everything I can do. I can drag stuff into the shadow, I can drag stuff out of the shadow, and I can hang out in your dreams. What was with that one last night, by the way? Who was that girl?"

"Eyes on the prize, Blot. If I give you the camera, would you be able to get it in there somehow?"

"If you're talking about another hug, I'm going to need some more time before I can do that again."

"No, no. Just you. You said you stole that money from my neighbor."

"That was just stretching. Shadows are good at stretching."

"So how far can you stretch?"

Blot gazed out the window. "I guess we'll find out."

Alan checked if the coast was clear, then stepped out of the car. He held the camera in hand. Tucked under his arm was a big three-battery D-cell flashlight. It was the kind of thing policemen shined into the eyes of suspicious motorists.

"Must you carry that thing?"

"I almost got killed by a shadow. I figure this is just basic self-defense. Think of it as a can of pepper spray for shades."

"Just don't use it on me."

"Sure thing. Now listen." He held up the camera, leaning over it to keep the worst of the rain from it. "This thing is really hard to use well, but really easy to do 'good enough' with."

He moved through the alleyways as stealthily as he could, making his way toward the warehouse where the meeting was taking place. As he did, he would pause in the shadows to provide Blot a bit more training. In fully automatic, the camera had really only one button Blot needed to know about, but he gave her as much of an education as he could manage in the time available. The camera was the same one he'd used for the time lapse. It was his most rugged and weather-resistant, so he wasn't *terribly* concerned about the rain, aside from how much it chilled him to the bone.

Soon they reached the dark alley beside the warehouse. Alan shut his eyes and strained his ears.

"I can just barely hear voices."

"There's two shades," she said quietly. "I can feel them. A couple of walls away."

He gazed up at the wall. "How are we going to get you in?"

Blot cast herself up along the wall; she tested every window and opening.

"They must be afraid of people like me. They've shaded all of the windows on the inside. I can't get through. But wait..."

She slid down and discovered a grating. It was the opening for a vent system, blocked by a heavy-duty mesh and a spinning fan.

"I can get through here," she said. "Why do you people *always* run these pipes and things through your buildings?"

"Usually, it's for air-conditioning."

"Well it's very useful." She snapped back down to his side.

"Okay, Blot. I need you to find them and record them without being seen. Remember, point the front part at them. I'm going to leave the screen off, but you'll see through here if it's pointed in the right direction."

"What about the flash?" she said.

"Forget about the flash. You don't need flash for video. And besides, if you use it, they'll notice you."

"Yeah, but if they notice me, I'll need to use it," she countered.

"Oh... Okay, that's fair. You twist this knob here, to this setting, then you hit this button and press that button there."

"Got it." She took a shaky breath. "How exactly is video and audio going to help again?"

"At the very least, it'll teach us what they're doing. And if there's one thing I've learned in my photographic career, it's that it never hurts to have footage of people doing something they shouldn't."

He held out the camera. She imitated his posture until it appeared she was holding its shadow. Then it simply lifted away from his hand.

"That is so weird..." he said, watching his camera drift up and away.

"It's about to get weirder," she warned.

The camera drifted over to the wall and lightly touched against it. Then, with a ripple of reality itself, it slipped through the wall, simply *becoming* its own shadow.

"Whoa..."

"Here goes nothing," she said. "If something looks like it is going to happen, I'm going to be right back here in a hurry. And you'd better let me know if something happens on your end."

149

"Are we going to be able to hear each other?"

"Of course." She pointed to his feet. "We'll still be connected. If you listen real close, you'll probably be able to hear what I hear."

"Will I be able to see what you see?"

"No so much. Not yet, anyway. Maybe in a few weeks."

She started to shift, her form stretching up along the wall as though a light was shifting down toward her feet and shining upward. When she reached the grating, she slid effortlessly inside.

Blot slid through the ventilation duct. The duct was roomy. Not that it needed to be for her to fit through it. If there was space to fit a sheet of paper through, there was room enough for her. It was also filthy, layered with rust, dust, and mold. Again, this was no concern to her. It was just a bit of extra texture for her to slide along.

She shut her eyes as she moved. She would be better served by her other senses. The shades she was after, though still only beginning to recover their strength, remained leagues ahead of her in power. She could feel them. It was an iciness in the distance, like hovering one's hand over a slab of metal brought in from the snow. Because they were so much more powerful than her, she knew there wasn't a chance they'd detect her in the same way. She was a single flake in the midst of a snowdrift.

The farther she stretched, the more effort it took to move. She could feel her connection to Alan grow thinner, but she pressed on. The back of her mind fluttered with doubt. No, she shouldn't be doing this. She shouldn't be helping a human in his attempts to foil her own kind. But that was not the source of her doubts. What concerned her was that below all of the logic and anxiety, she wasn't sure Alan was wrong. It was possible, just possible, that this was indeed what she should be doing. There may just be right and wrong after all. And what the other shades were doing was wrong, and what *she* was doing was right.

Blot tried to push that thought away. She didn't need that sort of confusion right now. This was Dun she was heading toward. He'd taught her. The things he and the others taught over a lifetime were the things she knew to be true. If they were wrong... where did that leave her?

No. This was about survival. It was simple as that. She had to do this, or it would be the end of her.

Another grating approached. It was above where she knew the others to be, but she wasn't confident she'd find a closer one. Blot squinted and slid through the grating. Sure enough, she was near the top of a tallish ceiling in one of the warehouse's inner chambers. Three men were below, or five, depending on how one counted. One pair was Lenny and Dun. Another was a normal human who looked thick as a side of beef. The last was another human afflicted with a shade, but she didn't recognize either of them.

The man was older. Maybe in his fifties. He was large. Not in a tall, muscular way like his associate. He was simply overall large. Six feet and change. Massive hands. Wide shoulders. He was from hearty stock. Thinning silver hair stood on his head in a crew cut, and his long jacket bore a vaguely military assortment of brass buttons and accents.

His shade was a hulk. While Dun was nearly the same size as her, this one was nearly a multiple of her size. He more closely resembled Blot's combat form than her normal one, and he was at rest. He was a soldier, not an instructor. She shuddered at the thought of what sort of tricks he might have learned.

She gathered her courage and let the camera ease out of the shadows. As high as she was, and as dim as the shades kept the room, there was little fear she'd be noticed. She depressed the button and gazed through the viewfinder to zoom in on them.

"Why does it shake so much?" she murmured to Alan.

"Did you find them?" he asked.

"Yes! But the view is very shaky."

"You're shaking."

"I'm not."

"It doesn't just shake on its own, Blot."

"*I'm not shaking,*" she insisted.

"Try leaning it on something."

She eased the camera against the edge of the vent. This proved to be a terrible mistake. The trembling camera rattled against the vent, and all eyes turned to her.

Blot hastily yanked the camera back into the shadows and looked desperately about.

"What was that?" Lenny said, peering into the darkness.

Blot's eyes came to rest on a rat dozing on a rafter ahead of her. She reached her hand out, stretching it almost to its limit, and nudged the creature. It released a startled squeal and scurried away.

"Never mind," rumbled the shade-afflicted stranger. "The sooner we get this over with, the sooner we can stop meeting in infested places like this. This isn't the sort of place a senate candidate should be seen."

"Did you hear that?" Blot said, easing the camera back out and directing it below.

"He's there? Commissioner Magnuson is there?" Alan said.

"I suppose. Or another one. How many senate candidates could there be?"

"Plenty. Are you recording?"

"Of course I'm recording."

"What have you got for me?" Commissioner Magnuson asked.

Lenny reached into his pocket and revealed a thumb drive. "This is pretty much everything I could find on the network." He glanced at the heavily armed man beside the commissioner. "Our, uh... mutual friend helped me get to basically the entire network."

"Before my people waste their time digging through this, is there anything good? Anything incriminating?"

Lenny scratched his head and glanced aside. "It's not... I mean, not really. Savage is pretty much on the up and up. The finance stuff is more or less transparent. No dark money I know of."

"No politician is completely clean." Commissioner Magnuson stuffed the drive in his pocket. "There'll be something."

"If nothing else, it'll have the ins and outs of their policy and stuff," Lenny said. "There's not much time left to make an impact, though."

"Oh, there's time. All it takes is something big. Something to put a stink on the man just as he's heading to the polls." Magnuson reached into the pocket of his jacket and fetched a thumb drive of his own. "Here."

Lenny took it. "What's this?"

"Let's just say that if that shows up in the possession of the campaign, Savage won't be able to deny those insider trading accusations any longer."

"You want me to slip this onto the network?"

"I'm just giving it to you. What you do with it is your own prerogative," Magnuson said.

The camera steadied slowly as the exchange continued. Blot chose to believe it was because whatever was causing it to tremble was finally subsiding. Surely it wasn't fear.

"This might actually work..." Blot murmured to Alan. "If you people really *are* ruled by laws, and this stuff really *is* illegal, then maybe we can get these people locked up. That wouldn't kill them, and surely The Dawn couldn't kill them if they were in jail."

"That's as good a plan as any. I... hold on, someone's coming. Get back here, quick. I think we've got to—"

Blot's eyes widened and she felt an irresistible tug toward Alan. It was all she could do to pull the camera back into the shadows before she was drawn back through the vent.

Alan squinted into the blinding light of a powerful lantern shining down the alley. He'd been listening so closely, trying to hear what Blot was hearing, that he'd not noticed a figure appear at one end of the alleyway until it was too late. Dazzled, he rushed away from the light and square into the chest of another man who'd been lying in ambush at the other end of the alley. A hand wrapped tightly around his shirt and shoved him against the wall of the warehouse. The man with the light rushed up. Alan tried to force his eyes open to identify his attackers, but there was no seeing past the punishing light.

A shadow swept in front of his eyes, and he could just make out the shape of a familiar pendant. It hung perfectly still and faced him directly. Or more accurately, it faced the two powerful shades hidden in the warehouse behind him.

"Ha! You again. I don't know how you hid yourself last time, but there's no denying it now," hissed the last voice in the world he'd wanted to hear.

It was The Dawn. The same two members he'd encountered in the parking structure.

"Alan, I can't move," Blot grunted.

"You've got to stop, guys!" Alan insisted. "You don't know what you're doing." He tried to force himself aside. The cultist held him still.

"There's no way we'd bump into you twice if you weren't part of it. You're coming with us."

The light-wielder kept the daylight-bright lantern in Alan's face as the other man wrenched his arm behind his back and forced him to walk toward the road.

"You've got to fight them, Alan. They'll kill us!" Blot urged.

Alan hadn't spontaneously developed any combat instincts since his last clash, and the astoundingly efficient armlock his assailant kept him in made it clear that The Dawn taught their people a thing or two about how to apprehend.

"Guys, you don't understand. Have you checked? There are guys with guns all over the—"

The man strong-arming him covered Alan's mouth. "You can do your talking when we tell you to. I caught hell for losing the blade. We've only got a couple of recovery guys, you know. You should've left the knife where it fell. Now we know where you live."

They pitched him headlong into what turned out to be the empty back of a windowless contractor's van. The moment his face hit the cold metal of the floor, floodlights snapped on to keep him bathed in brilliance from all sides. One man climbed in with him to keep him restrained. The other rushed around to the driver's seat. Outside, Alan heard raised voices shouting orders. The heavies the commissioner had on watch had come to inspect the unexplained blaring lights.

"Go, go, go!" commanded the man binding Alan's wrists.

The van's wheels squealed against the wet cement of the alleyway, and they lurched aside. It was a wonder the van didn't flip. Without his hands free, Alan fell aside and smashed his face on the wall of the van. For the second time in his life, and the second time in a week, a blow to his head left him dazed and disoriented, unable to resist as he was hauled away.

By the time Alan's brain was back in working order, he was tied to a chair. A bright light shone from behind him, plastering Blot on the floor before him. She stared up at him, terrified. Every few moments she shuddered and trembled, trying to fight the influence of the light, but it was no use.

Footsteps echoed around him. The contrast of light and dark made it difficult to see the room outside the pool of light, but he could hear footsteps and hushed conversation. From the echoes, the room felt small and empty.

Someone stepped into the edge of the light, carefully clear of his shadow. It wasn't one of the pair that had kidnapped him. This was a much older man. He leaned on a silver-headed, silver-tipped cane. Spectacles with round lenses sat on a narrow nose. He squinted at the bright light, then flipped down a second set of lenses, sunglasses hinged to the top of his eyeglasses.

The man leaned a bit more heavily on the cane to free a hand to reach to a table just outside the pool of light.

"Alan Fontaine," he said, eying the driver's license he plucked up. "Not exactly a spy, are you, Alan? Lots of information about you here."

"Listen. You have to believe me. I'm not what you think I am. This isn't what you think it is."

"I don't have to believe you, Alan. See, people are liars. Especially people who are trapped. Cornered." He glanced at someone in the darkness.

One of the two members of The Dawn that had apprehended Alan appeared. He set down what looked like a pie tin, centered at right about chest level in the shadow.

"No, no, no, no..." murmured Blot, eyes wide and fearful.

"Please. Just listen. I'm telling you—" Alan began.

"I am *talking*," the old man said, punctuating the outburst with a sharp clack of the cane's head on the cement floor of the room. It missed Blot by mere inches. She flinched as though she'd felt it.

"That cane, Alan. It's like the knives..." she said coldly.

"Where was I?" the old man said. "Alan here derailed the old train of thought."

"Lies, keeper," said the younger man, who returned with a bag of kitty litter.

"Right, right. Lies." He paced past his subordinate as litter was poured into the pie tin. "See, you're going to lie to me. No right-minded man in your situation wouldn't. You're going to say whatever you think will get you out of here alive. If you think I'll let you go if you claim this shadow here is the one you were born with, you'll swear it up, down, left, right, and center. You'll lie and lie and lie."

The other man cleared away, and the old man stepped up to the pie tin. He gazed aside at Alan.

"But you know what won't lie?" He raised his cane. "This."

He thrust it down, digging its tip into the kitty litter. Blot screeched in agony. She shuddered and struggled. The pan slid about beneath her. Alan released a ragged breath. He couldn't feel the attack himself, not precisely. But there was a sudden coldness, a hollowness in the pit of his stomach. It was like a part of him had gone numb the moment the man attacked.

A smile of achievement stretched the wizened face of the old man. Square white teeth, the sort of grin one gets from cheap dentures, gleamed in the light.

"Oh, you've got one of them clinging to you, Alan. I knew this old trick would work." He leaned a bit harder and Blot shrieked. "You're supposed to use ashes from burnt mistletoe, but anything sandy works in a pinch. Just so long as the head of the cane has something to sink into—" He twisted the head. Blot's howls of pain stung Alan's ears. "You can punch right through," he finished.

Alan turned his head aside. "Please! Don't hurt her."

"Don't hurt *her*." The old man leaned closer, putting some more pressure on the cane in the process. "You got a lady, have you?"

"Don't tell him anything!" Blot cried, trying to fight her way through the pain. "We're both dead. There's no way either of us survive."

"Alan, I don't know what lies this thing has whispered in your ear. But the shades have only the darkest of intentions. You can help us stop them."

"I won't help you kill people."

The old man raised his eyebrows. "Kill people? We are saving lives, Alan. Don't you want to help defend your world?"

"You are going to kill the shades, and you are going to kill the people whom they're clinging to."

"We are going to stop the bleeding. We are going to wipe out the infection before it spreads. Though it is refreshing that you know that your life and the life of this one are linked. You'll know just what this means."

He nodded at someone in the darkness. Alan heard the scrape of metal on stone. Slowly, the light began to move. Blot followed the light, skewing aside. But with the cane pinning her in place, the motion started to tug and tear at her. She shrieked anew, her form twisting and shifting. Glimmers of light appeared around the tip of the cane, like she was formed of fabric that was beginning to tear. The terrifying, icy numbness in the pit of Alan's stomach grew. He could see her beginning to peel away.

"Talk. Maybe we'll lock you up instead. No sense killing a good source of information."

"You're a monster," Alan breathed.

A cold sweat was running down his forehead now; phantom numbness was beginning to coil up his legs. He could see Blot trying to take on her combat form, but the light was too bright, the cane too painful. Her features simply shifted and trembled. The concrete beneath her gouged with the scrabbling claws pulled back behind her in imitation of Alan's bound position.

"Bring it in," the old man said. "If he actually cares for his little parasite, maybe he'll have a change of heart if her features are large as life."

The light shifted back, then started to get closer. Blot struggled and screamed as the approaching light caused her to cover more of the floor, stretching her away from where she was pinned. Alan tried to huddle down, to keep her form from tugging too terribly against the cane.

"Stop this!" Alan demanded.

"Start talking. A word of help is all it will take to ease her suffering."

"He'll kill us all!" Blot cried. "Die like a warrior, Alan. Don't give him what he wants."

The coldness in him was spreading. Behind him, he could feel the intensity of the light on the back of his head. If he didn't do something, Blot would be torn free. She'd simply be killed, and he wouldn't last much longer. A desperate thought came to mind. He heaved himself back. His head smashed against the light. It shattered, flashed, and sent the room into jet blackness.

"Blot! Can you escape?" he grunted, shaking broken glass from his hair.

"I can't... I'm... still pinned..." She wheezed. "But maybe I can do something."

In the darkness, slashing and grinding mixed with startled cries.

"Get some lights on, idiots!" commanded the old man.

The overhead lights clicked on. Alan was briefly treated to a glimpse of Blot, halfway between her combat and true shape. One hand was clawing at the leg of the old man who had her pinned. The other was slashing through the air. One of the other henchmen was backed against a wall, clutching an arm with some superficial scratch marks.

When the light snapped on, Blot was once again tugged toward the position a proper shadow should have been. As the bulb was directly overhead, she should have shot under Alan's chair, but the cane still had her pinned. She ended up doubled over the silver tip of the weapon, clawing and heaving at it like an impaled vampire. The overhead light wasn't nearly as strong, and she could at least struggle against its influence. If not for that small mercy, she likely would have been shredded by the sudden motion.

"Get another job light in here," the old man ordered. "I don't like how this one is fighting. We need something brighter."

"I can't... I can't..." Blot breathed weakly.

She reached up with shaking hands. She was at the end of her rope. Alan's eyes desperately swept over the now fully illuminated room. The table formerly hidden in the darkness was just beside the old man. It was scattered with the contents of Alan's pockets, including one gleaming object.

"Blot! The table!" he barked.

She didn't even open her tightly shut eyes. Her quivering hand lashed up and caught the shadow of the table's leg. With a desperate pull, she caused it to barely shudder. It wasn't much, but it was enough. The table slid a few inches, and Alan's personal effects rattled a bit. A small, silver bell rolled to the edge and tumbled to the ground.

When it struck, it produced a single clear chime. The pristine sound was still hanging in the air when there came a rapid, purposeful knock.

All eyes rose to the door, still open from the lackey heading out to fetch a replacement light. A pair of figures were standing in the doorway. Both in white-on-white suits. Both with bizarre opaque white sunglasses.

"You rang, Mr. Fontaine?" said Dina.

For a moment that felt like a lifetime, all froze and stared at the newcomers.

"Gentlemen, if you'll excuse us, we need the room for a moment," Gabriel said.

"Who are you?" The old man said the words warily, but not nearly as warily as he should have considering two uninvited guests had appeared without explanation.

"We are from the front office, and we need a few minutes alone with this individual," Gabriel said.

The old man flipped up the dark lenses of his glasses and gave them a suspicious look.

"Now, please," Dina said.

"You heard them, boys," the old man said. "Damn front office can't leave us to do our job."

The old man lifted the cane from the tin of litter. Blot immediately slid beneath the chair. It was where the light dictated she should be, but the way she slumped there, she looked as though she was cowering.

"Well, well, well," Dina said. "You seem to have gotten yourself into something of a pickle, Alan."

"You guys are working with The Dawn after all?"

"Heavens no, Alan. Whatever gave you that idea?" said Gabriel.

"You said you were from the front office."

"As a rule, cults do not have a front office. One of their few redeeming characteristics is a glorious absence of bureaucracy," Dina said.

"With one or two notable exceptions," Gabriel said.

Dina looked to her associate. "Once they attain tax-exempt status, I think we can leave the cult terminology behind." She looked back to Alan. "A rare point of disagreement between the two of us."

"Can you untie me? This is all a misunderstanding," Alan said.

"Is it a misunderstanding, Alan?" Dina said. "To be sure of that, we'll need to determine just what the understanding is."

Blot curled a little more tightly under the chair.

"Why do I get the feeling I've just traded one interrogation for another?" Alan said.

"Because you have been given the gift of insight, Alan," Gabriel said.

"The charitable thing to do would be to share that enlightenment," Dina added.

They stood on either side of the unassuming pie tin that had been used to nearly execute Blot and Alan.

"Let us begin with the determinations you have made about your condition."

"I... I'll tell you what I told them. I don't want anyone killed. I won't tell you any names."

"I don't believe we asked for names, Alan," Dina said.

"Tell us what you have learned about your condition," Gabriel said.

"It's a shade," he said, as though the question had levered his mind open and pried the answer out. "My shadow has been pulled free and replaced by a shade. If anything happens to either of us, we both die."

"Concisely put," Gabriel said.

"Typically, someone in your position would be either oblivious to that fact or actively involved in the plots of the similarly afflicted. But not you. How curious," Dina added.

"Who are you people?"

"Presently, we are the sort of people who ask questions, not the sort who answer them," Gabriel replied.

"Here is what you need to know, Alan," Dina said. "We aren't on your side. We aren't on the side of the shades. We aren't on the side of The Dawn. For the moment, think of us as..."

"Referees?" Gabriel offered.

"Yes. Near enough for our present purposes. For the moment, we are here to ensure that no one strays too far from the rules of play." She leaned forward. "And you are playing rather erratically."

"I'm just trying to survive," Alan said.

"Demonstrably untrue," Gabriel said.

"Lurking in the alley, eavesdropping on the political intrigue of two shades and their hosts. These are not the actions of a man focused on survival."

"I told you..." Blot said.

"How long have you been watching me?" he said.

"Need we reestablish the direction of the flow of information yet again, Alan?" Dina asked.

"I'm just trying to do the right thing, okay?"

Dina raised her eyebrows. "That much rings true."

"Many foolish and self-destructive mistakes have been made in the name of 'the right thing,'" Gabriel observed.

"We are accustomed to antagonistic relationships between shade and host," Dina said. "They tend to be brief, and to end it the death of both."

"We are similarly familiar with mutually beneficial relationships between shade and host," Gabriel said. "They tend to bend in the direction of global domination, in whatever small way they can."

"I'm getting a little uncomfortable that my role has been reduced to 'host,'" Alan said. "Can we at least call me 'human'?"

"If you think that will somehow improve your situation, certainly," Dina said.

"But it doesn't change the fact that your specific relationship is different from what we've come to anticipate," Gabriel said.

"Quite rare."

"Unprecedented, in our admittedly less-than-comprehensive experience."

Dina leaned forward. "We don't fully understand it, Alan. And as a result, we don't *like* it."

"So help us understand," Gabriel said simply.

"Blot is a good person," Alan said. "I don't want her to die. But I don't want her people to take things over. But I don't want *them* to die."

"You have a variety of desires that are thoroughly at odds," Dina said.

"If you were not bound to that chair, if you'd not been caught, and if things had gone your way, what precisely would you be doing presently? What would be your ideal outcome?"

"Stop the plan, save the lives."

"But *how*?"

"However I can."

Both of the associates took a step back, looking him up and down in unison. They turned to each other.

"I would say he is going to be a brief but fascinating anomaly," Dina said.

"Something worthy of observation," Gabriel said.

They both nodded.

"Carry on," they said together.

Gabriel plucked the silver bell from the table and slipped it into Alan's jacket pocket. Then both approached the door.

"Aren't you going to at least let me go?" Alan said.

"Now that wouldn't be terribly impartial, would it?" Dina said.

"Consider this a time out. Play shall resume momentarily," Gabriel said.

"But Alan..." Dina put her fingers to her sunglasses and slid them down enough to glance over them. A warm, piercing glow issued forth from within, bright enough to force Alan to turn his head. Blot rushed across the room and pinned herself against the far wall like a bug pressed beneath a pane of glass. "We will be watching you."

They opened the door. The cultists were standing outside, their gazes vacant.

"As you were, gentlemen," Dina said.

As the white-suited pair left the room, there was a moment of peace. Every mind within range of them sluggishly came to and attempted to pick up where it had left off. Questions of what precisely had just happened rose up but were brushed aside. Eyes blinked. People looked at one another. Half-formed sentences started and stopped. The first person to recover sufficiently was Blot, followed swiftly by Alan as he felt clawed fingers rake through the rope securing his hands.

"Why is he alone in there?" barked the old man. "Get in there."

Alan shot from the chair and scooped the contents of the table into his bag, which was splayed open after being emptied. Aside from his own things, there were a few tools of the trade and documents left behind by The Dawn that might prove useful.

Blot gathered herself and rose up out of the shadows, twisted and contorted into as near a warrior's form as she could muster. It was hardly intimidating. Smaller than Alan, she looked like a scrawny, clawed goblin. A ragged hole had been torn through her abdomen where the cane had jabbed her. It hung in tatters like cloth. From the reaction of The Dawn, her rising up out of the shadows was enough for even those free of the influence of their own shade to see her. Intimidating or no, the sight of an ink-black being looming up from the ground was enough to unnerve them. The man who had been sent to fetch the replacement interrogation light dove to plug it in. Blot slashed, smashing the light. Another member of The Dawn clicked on a handheld spot, and she struck the far wall hard enough to buckle the paneling.

"I can't... The lights..." she croaked.

Alan's instincts told him to run screaming before he got hurt, but the only way out was forward, through the gathered members of The Dawn. He was cornered. And since the beginning of time, a cornered creature had always been a dangerous one. The same desperation-fueled frenzy that would have sent him sprinting away turned into a charging tackle to the man with the light. They tumbled to the ground. The man lost the light, but it was a rugged piece of hunting gear and stubbornly refused to break. Alan's adrenaline-fueled struggle eventually gave him the upper hand, and he rolled free and grabbed the light. When he staggered to his feet, he found he was surrounded. There were at least six Dawn members, not counting the old man. Not knowing what else to do, he flashed the light toward them, sweeping it back and forth across their faces as he backed toward a door he hoped would lead outside. They squinted and flinched, but one by one they donned darker glasses.

"Of course they'd be ready for that..." he moaned.

"What are we going to do?" Blot said, looming behind him but fighting to maintain her physicality. "There's too many of them."

"I... uh..." He looked over his shoulder to her. "I apologize for this."

He spun the light around. Blot launched back, smashing the door before her combat form gave way to a massless silhouette again. Alan ran in a blind sprint, desperate to reach freedom.

He burst out of a doorway into the drizzling rain. For all of the misfortune they'd had thus far, luck was with them in that The Dawn weren't a well-staffed or well-armed force. There were eight of them total in the whole building, and now all were far behind him. Some had felt the scattered slashes of Blot when she could gather herself enough to rise up again. Most had stumbled and tripped as Alan, now in the more familiar ground of a full retreat, pulled down every possible obstacle along the way to trip them up.

He tossed the stolen light aside and tried to blink away the spots consuming his vision. The escape had brought him to a drenched back alley, the sort of place tucked behind strip malls and office parks to allow goods to be loaded without taking up precious parking. It was poorly lit and largely deserted, save for the van that had brought him here and a Dawn cultist behind the wheel.

The man released a startled yelp as he saw Alan dash toward him. He jabbed the key into the ignition, but before he could turn it and activate the headlights, Blot streaked up to him and reached a claw in through the window. It passed easily through, despite the fact that the window was shut. She raked a semisubstantial hand along the door to pop it open, then snagged his shirt and dragged him to the ground. Once he was down, she peeled herself up enough to loom weakly over him. Her hands trembled against the ground on either side of his head as she gazed down with piercing white eyes.

"Look what your people did to me..." she seethed, glancing down at the ragged hole. She raised a hand and, with supreme effort, lengthened its fingers into claws. "Let's see how *you* like it..."

"Blot, no!" Alan shouted as he heaved an empty trash bin to block the door.

She turned from the trembling man. "Fair is fair, Alan."

"An eye for an eye just keeps the chain of violence going." He glanced back over his shoulder. "Come on, we've got to get out of here."

Alan pushed past her and hopped into the driver's seat. Blot eyed the struggling cultist.

"Your wallet," she said.

"Wh-what?" the cultist said.

"Give me your wallet!" she shouted, holding one hand out and pressing the other to his chest. "And your phone, too."

"I'll never submit to a—"

Blot shut her eyes and pressed on his chest. The ground beneath him started to ripple. He started to slide into the shadows. The supernatural chill of it, combined with not truly knowing what might happen to him, changed the cultist's tune. With trembling hands, he emptied his pockets into her open hand. She closed the items in her grip, and they vanished into her shadowy form.

"What's the password?" she barked.

"What are you—" the cultist said.

She pushed harder. "For the phone! The password!"

"It's just a square!" he yelped.

Alan turned the keys. The engine revved up. Some of the other members of The Dawn arrived at the doorway. Blot released the pressure. The terrified man "surfaced." She leaned down, face-to-face with him.

"Remember that I let you live," she fumed.

With that, she released a breath and let her physical form drop away. She swiftly slid along the ground, up the side of the van, and in beside Alan. He performed one of the more graceless K-turns of his life and slung some icy slush from the alley floor as he floored the accelerator and squealed out into city streets.

It took five minutes of driving as recklessly as he could bring himself to before Alan could convince himself the cultists weren't on his tail. Thirty seconds of hindsight reminded him there weren't any other vehicles in the alley, so it was very possible they didn't have the means to make chase at all. At least not immediately.

He blinked away the frigid rain that still ran down his forehead and numbed his face and risked a glance down at the shadow that was peeking out from behind him.

"Are you okay?"

"I'm cold," Blot murmured. "And I'm tired. And I hurt. But I'm not dead."

He felt motion behind him and then a light slap at the back of his head.

"What was that business with the light? Thumping me into the door like a club!"

"I didn't know what else to do. I'm so sorry. Are you okay?"

"I already said I am."

"What do we do now?" he said.

"I don't know. Just... drive. Find somewhere safe."

He took a breath. "I'm not sure there is such a place..."

Chapter 7

Alan shivered in the rain beside a bus stop. He'd driven to an overnight parking lot to stash the van. The last thing he wanted was for a stolen vehicle to be waiting out in front of his apartment where the cops could find it and question him about it. But that meant taking mass transit home.

"You can stand in the bus stop," Blot said.

He shook his head. "There's a light. You'd be stuck."

"It's not that bright."

"You're hurt and you're tired and you need to recover. I'll stay in the dark for as long as I can."

"If you really want me to recover, you could get some more coffee."

He released a near-laugh. "What is it with you and coffee?"

"What? It makes me feel better."

"I still wonder where you put it all. If it goes in, it's got to go out, right?"

"Are you sure the body functions of metaphysical beings are really the subject you want to discuss right now?"

The bus turned the corner and approached.

"What I'd *like* to discuss right now is where I can get a nice club sandwich. Some well-done fries. A full-sour pickle. Maybe where I could see a movie," he said. "You'd like seeing movies. Nice, dark room. Plenty of interesting things to look at. But I *can't* discuss that, because instead we have to discuss what we're going to do about the many, many people who want us dead."

The bus stopped and Alan stepped on. He fished in his pockets and discovered that, if he had any money at all, it had been lost in his shoulder bag after he swept the contents of the interrogation table into it. He felt something damp pressed into his palm. Blot had passed him the stolen wallet. He glanced up to the bus driver to see if he'd seen it, but the man had the sort of dead-eyed stare that suggested he hadn't seen anything since 1995. Alan found a couple of singles and shoved them into the bill collector, then hobbled down the bus walkway as it continued on its route.

"So what do we do?" Alan said. He plopped down in a seat in the back, beneath a broken light.

"Are you sure we can talk? There are people around."

"We're on a bus, late at night, in Philadelphia. A soaking-wet maniac arguing quietly with his shadow isn't going to turn any heads."

"If you say so." She slid up the wall beside him. "I think we should probably take some time to figure out what our problems really are."

"Right... Right, let's see..."

"Okay, okay, you can stop," Blot said quietly.

In retrospect, attempting to list the depths of the catastrophe they found themselves in may not have been the best way to cope with the latest near-death experience. Whatever instinctive layer of abstraction had kept Alan from plunging into the swirling depths of panic and despair had shattered under the weight of the reality he was presently plumbing.

"...except we can't go there, because the family doesn't *own* that anymore. If you don't recover, then we'll both die. If you do recover, then eventually you'll get strong enough that The Dawn will be able to track us down, and then we'll both die. And if we don't, then somewhere in the background your brethren are going to wrap their claws around the people who run things, and if Dun is any indication, that's not going to go well for the rest of humanity, and if we don't do anything, then maybe The Dawn will massacre all of those people. We'll probably end up in a police state, what with there being a massive coordinated attempt to kill world leaders. And then people will start investigating, and if they don't find out it was the shades, then you folks will still be in charge, and if they do, then the cops will be after me too..."

Blot gazed past him at the rest of the passengers. "No one is even looking," she said. "And that man over there is clipping his toenails. You were right. I don't think you are the craziest person on the bus."

"I just don't think there's any way we're going to get out of this alive."

"I suggest we find a dark place far away and stay there. I'll try to practice hiding myself. If I get good enough at it, then we can probably last for quite a while."

"But that doesn't solve any of the other problems."

"We've got enough of our own problems to be solving other people's problems."

"That's not how the world is supposed to work. We're supposed to—*holy hell!*"

Alan nearly threw himself into the aisle of the bus as a sudden noise erupted from his bag. It took a repetition of the sound before he realized it was his ringtone. He shakily pulled the phone out and answered without checking the number.

"Hello?" he said.

"Alan?" said the voice on the other side.

It was Jessie, his friend at the police station.

"Oh, hey. Hey, Jessie." He wiped his face. "What's up?"

"You sound terrible, Alan. Is something wrong?"

He grappled with what if anything would adequately explain the frazzled state of his mind and voice to her. She wouldn't believe the truth, and he didn't want to burden her with it. His mental capacity wasn't up to the task of fabricating a worthwhile story.

He settled on, "I got caught in the rain."

"I'm not surprised. We've got your car here."

"... My car?"

"Yeah. It just got impounded. At first I wasn't sure it was yours, because why the heck would you be parked at some warehouse? But I recognize your bumper stickers. That and we ran the plates."

"That was quick." He rubbed his head. "Or was it? I guess I could have lost a chunk of the day."

"How exactly would you lose a chunk of the day?"

"Just... busy. What do I do now?"

"You've got to come down and pick it up. I'll see if I can get some of the fines knocked off."

"Yeah... Yeah, I guess I'll get down there. It might take me a while. I'm on the wrong bus for that."

"Why are you on the bus? You could just get a cab or ride-share or whatever."

"That'd cost five times as much, and I've got fines to pay, right?"

"That doesn't explain why you were already on the bus when I called."

"It's... I didn't think about that. I guess I just wanted to be alone for a minute."

"On the bus."

"You been on a bus lately? There is no place lonelier than a bus."

"If you say so, Alan. Give me a call when you get close. I'll have them buzz you in. Hey, maybe I can introduce you to the guy who does the hiring for the Forensic Division."

"I'm not really in 'interview' shape at the moment, Jessie."

"The guy spends most of his day taking photos of dead bodies. You don't need a suit and tie."

"Heh. You haven't seen me lately. But I guess I'll be there as soon as I can regardless. Thanks, by the way. I appreciate you keeping an eye out for my car." He glanced to the bag. "Oh, and I might have some questions for you when I get there. Legal stuff."

"Oh, no problem. See you in a bit."

He hung up and tapped through to his map application to figure out where to change buses for the police station.

"You wanted to be alone?" Blot said.

"I guess. Kinda. You know. To think. I wanted a place where someone else wouldn't talk to me."

"Should I not talk to you?"

"No, that's not..." He shook his head again, his wits very gradually slipping back into a nonpanicked configuration. "I'm sorry. I'll have to try to remember I'm part of a duo now."

"You spend a lot of time apologizing to people. People whom you really shouldn't be apologizing to. I *am* the reason all of this started for you."

"It wasn't your fault."

"Any reasonable person would agree that I am one hundred percent at fault for the mess of your life right now. It's mostly your fault that you've nearly gotten us killed since then, but I'm the reason you're in the mess you're in."

"Maybe so, but it's not a nice thing to say." He perused the info on the phone. "Three more stops and we'll change at Morris Street. How's your, uh... hole?"

She slid up along the wall and gazed down along herself. The wound was still plainly visible. "It's bad. Not fatal, but it'll be days before I'm healed up."

"Days? Really? Only a few days to heal a gaping chest wound?"

"Yeah. How long does it take you to heal from a hole like that?"

"I'm pretty sure it would kill me."

"Really? They never really talked about how flimsy you people are. Fortunately, the cane didn't hit the camera."

"The camera?" He looked in his bag and discovered, to his dismay, the device was not present. "Where is it?"

She raised her hand, now holding the silhouette of his DSLR. "I still have it."

Her shadowy hand slid down to his bag. The damp canvas plumped up a bit with the form of the camera sliding into reality again. Despite all of the combat and calamity, it was spotless and untouched. It wasn't even wet.

"Where was it this whole time? I didn't see you holding it."

"Shadows don't have any depth. We can stack stuff pretty deep."

He picked it up. "It's still recording."

"I didn't exactly have the chance to turn it off. You're lucky I didn't end up dropping it in the warehouse."

He hit stop and switched to review mode. The camera didn't have any speakers on it, and he didn't feel like finding his earbuds, but a bit of skipping around revealed that Blot's camera work was about as good as one could expect from someone who had only known that cameras existed for less than a week. The video continued while it was in shadow, presenting the same mind-bending version of reality that Alan had briefly endured. A dancing waveform at the bottom suggested the audio had continued recording as well. "Interesting... Knowing electronics still do their job while you've got them tucked away has promise. But that'll have to wait. We're going to be walking into a police station in a couple of minutes. We've got between now and then to get me looking like someone they shouldn't immediately lock up."

The lights flickered on in a dusty conference room. A young woman with black hair and a crisp police uniform leaned in.

"Yeah, this'll be fine," Jessie said.

She stepped inside. Alan followed. The light was bright enough that Blot had limited mobility, but that was just as well. With Jessie around, Alan would have to pretend his shadow was just a shadow.

"Here's the paperwork," she said, flopping down a few sheets of paper. She pulled a pen from her shirt pocket and handed it to him.

"Man, I never realized how many old-fashioned forms you had to fill out to get stuff done with the police," Alan said. "Between this and the break-in."

"Yeah, what was the deal with that?" she said. "You didn't really tell me the details."

"It wasn't much. Jeez. I forgot to fill those forms out."

"Sounds like you've been having a rough time lately." She leaned forward. "And you've got some really nasty bumps."

"Yeah... Did I tell you I got fired from Cox Media?"

"No, really?" she said. "You been breaking mirrors or something? You've really got a cloud hanging over you lately."

"Yeah..." He started scratching down information on the sheet, but paused. "Jessie... Can you keep a secret?"

She raised an eyebrow. "That's not really the kind of question you ask a cop."

"I'm asking you in the context of a friend from college."

"Oh, well in that case," she sat down opposite him, "dish."

"Forgive me if this is a little choppy," he said. "Names changed to protect the innocent and all that."

"Sure, sure."

"The thing that got me fired was a snafu regarding the festival charity auction. But while I was there, I got some shots of an intern."

"Uh-huh."

"I…" He paused to choose his words carefully. "I've crossed paths with that intern a couple of times since then. I think he might be up to no good."

"What kind of no good?"

"Uh… Let's call it 'electoral shenanigans.'"

"I see."

"I think something is about to go down. Something might hit the news. And it's possible this kid might be involved."

"Do you have evidence?"

He leaned forward. "What sort of evidence would it take?"

She leaned back and gazed up.

"That's a tricky one. Just whom are we talking about getting taken down? Is this the intern taking down a candidate? Is this the intern getting taken down?"

"Anything. What would it take in an electoral shenanigans situation to have the cuffs thrown on someone?"

"Oh. A full arrest. And on short notice. There's any number of things. Most of the political stuff doesn't lead to cuffs until there's an investigation."

"I get the feeling an investigation won't bear fruit until…" Again he paused. "It'll take too long, let's put it that way."

Jessie drummed her fingers on the desk and glanced from side to side. She leaned close and whispered, "Are we talking about the senate race?"

"Maybe."

"And are we talking about Commissioner Magnuson?"

"He might be involved."

"As the target of the shenanigans?"

"Possibly the other side."

She sucked her teeth. "You'd better be careful whom you say that to."

"Hence the 'can you keep a secret' preamble."

"The old commish is well-liked and well-connected around here. First-name basis with half the force. It'll be tough to get anyone to take allegations against him seriously enough to act on it."

"What about video?" he said.

"Of what?"

He leaned down to his bag and produced his camera. "You didn't see this," he said.

He started the video file Blot had taken. Jessie watched it, face impassive. While she did, he fished out an earbud to listen to the audio with her. This was the first time he was hearing the footage from Blot's inaugural usage of the camera. Even with the audio, it wasn't Pulitzer Prize quality, to put it lightly. Most of the time, the meeting taking place was near the corner of the frame, if it was visible at all. The audio was coherent, but so buried in echoes that one would be hard-pressed to identify anyone by voice.

"I take it you didn't record this?" Jessie said. "Or you recorded it with your feet."

Blot muttered something.

"Never mind who recorded it. Hypothetically, could this put someone behind bars?"

She sighed. "Let me see it again."

He played it back. Her doubtful expression didn't improve.

"There are problems. It probably wouldn't stand up in court. Plenty of plausible deniability about who exactly we're looking at. Then there's the matter of the legality of *getting* the footage. This might, *might*, justify a warrant or something, if it was anyone but the commish. But it *is* the commish. So I'd suggest you hold on to that, because handing it over is liable to get it tucked into an evidence locker and forgotten. If you wanted to torpedo an election, this leaking to the news would probably do it. But a court of law has higher standards than the court of public opinion. Usually, anyway."

"So tell me what *would* get the cuffs on these guys."

"A clear and obvious crime taking place, with witnesses besides a shaky camera. If it was something that might place people in danger, even better." She frowned. "Not that placing people in danger is good, but it is grounds for immediate arrest."

He nodded and stowed his camera before running his hands through his still-damp hair. Jessie looked him over.

"Man, you really are beat up." She brushed his hair back to reveal the bruises left by his many recent knocks to the noggin. "This really looks bad. And your eyes are twitchy."

"The twitchiness is just nerves," he said. "Or... maybe that thing football players get from concussions."

"CTE?"

"That's it. Can you get that in a weekend?"

"I think it's more of a career thing. You been taking shots to the head regularly?"

"I've been clumsy," he said flatly.

"I think maybe you were right. Now might not be the time to meet with our forensics guy. But if you need help, don't hesitate to call me, okay?"

"Yeah. I might be taking you up on that," he said.

She tapped the form. "Fill those out. I'll get the ball rolling on getting your car out of impound."

It took two more hours, but he eventually got to his parking structure in his own car. He was a mess. His bag was a mess. And when he opened the door to his apartment, it was still in a bit of a mess from what he'd not yet cleaned up when The Dawn had ransacked it. He shut the door behind him and set down a pair of large black coffees from Vice Versa. The very moment she was certain she was unobserved, Blot darted to hers and slurped at the straw.

"I'm still not sure it's a good idea to come back here. The Dawn *and* the white suits know where you live," Blot said.

He rolled his head and listened to the soft crackle of a badly abused neck. "What am I going to do? Stay at a friend's house and get them involved? At least this will contain the blast radius of this bomb that's gone off in my life," he said and started mechanically cleaning up the rest of the mess.

"I take from all those questions that you're still convinced there's some way you're going to bring justice to Dun and whomever he was working with."

"I sort of assume I'll bring justice to the humans, and the shades'll just have to deal with it."

"So what are your ideas?"

"I don't know... Maybe we do like Jessie said. Leak the video to the press."

"Or sell it," Blot suggested. "You said that sort of thing was valuable."

"That feels scummy, to make money off this."

She slurped a bit more. "If you're going to face off against these people, you're going to be traipsing through the mud. There's no way you're coming out of it without getting scummy. If you ask me, I say we should lean into it."

"Lean into it?"

"You're playing this like if you just follow the rules hard enough, they'll just give up and turn themselves in. That's not how it works. The only thing we've got that is even a step in the right direction is that video, and you only got *that* by doing what I think you'd call 'breaking and entering.'"

He slid a dislodged drawer back into his end table. "We didn't have to break to enter."

"The point is, you're waiting for them to fall into a trap, but you don't get someone to fall into a trap by setting it and waiting. You need *bait*. You need to lie, cheat, steal, and bluff. You need to get them into a corner so tight, the only way out of it is to step right into that trap. Or you've got to put down something so juicy, so perfect, so irresistible that they can't help but throw themselves into your trap. You need to play dirty."

"I'm not any good at playing dirty, though."

She smiled wide and rubbed her hands together. "Lucky for you I was *trained* for that sort of thing."

He looked at her sideways. "You're seeming a little more eager about this than you have been."

"Look, I'm *also* trained to be observant. I'm supposed to watch for patterns, to learn how things work. And so far it's pretty clear you're just going to keep flinging us into the business end of a machine built to chew us up and spit us out. I'm not going to be able to stop you. So I can at least try to work out how to keep you from getting us killed." She looked away. "And besides. We're a team now. Our own team. The shades won't want me. I couldn't control you, and when it came down to it, I chose you over Dun. That's an executable offense. So you're all I've got. *We* are all I've got."

"All things being equal, you're probably wishing you ended up with someone who was less of a Boy Scout."

"I don't know. You're not what I was taught to hope for, but..." She glanced to the dimmed light overhead. "The first thing you did when you came into a wrecked house, even while the white-suits were here, was dim the lights for me. You've been stubbing your toe on tables and wandering around in half darkness because you know it'll make me more comfortable. I think the reason they don't teach us to hope for a host like this is because it's just too much to hope for. That Lenny guy will do whatever Dun tells him because he wants the wealth and power Dun promises and he doesn't want to have his head crushed like a melon. You do what I ask because you are... *nice*. You fight for me because you don't want *me* to die, not because you don't want *you* to die. And... it makes me want to do the same."

"Aw... You big softy."

"Now's no time for soft, Alan. There are dirty doings to be done. First things first. For both Lenny and that commissioner guy, I guarantee you the shade is calling the shots. So we shouldn't be thinking about what it takes to entice a human. This is a time to think about what it takes to entice a shade."

"Which is?"

She slid across the room to his bag and pulled out the phone and wallet she'd stolen from the cultist.

"Information about our enemies." She handed him the phone. "Open it up! The password is a square. Whatever that means."

He pressed the power button and started sweeping across the grid it presented. It took a few tries to figure out where to start the square, but once he did, the phone unlocked.

"How did you know to take the phone? And to ask for the code to open it?"

"Like I said, they teach us to observe. Even the weakest shade can still help the cause just by *watching*. They drilled that into me because... well... I'm pretty much the weakest shade. And you're *always* using your phone, and you always enter 7854 to unlock it."

"Hey, keep it down with that."

"So I figure The Dawn probably have a lot of important stuff on their phones."

He tapped his way through screens and thumbed his way through applications. "This feels wrong."

"It *is* wrong. But it's the wrong path to the right thing. So what has he got?" she asked, looking over his shoulder.

"I mean... exactly what you'd want. Names, locations. But are you suggesting we turn this information over to the shades?"

"No! I suggest we *offer* to hand this information over. This is the bait. Trust me, it'll have Dun and anyone else *salivating*. Knowing who the members of The Dawn are? Maybe learning enough to get to the root of the group and snuff them out? It'll push everything else aside."

"But what sort of a trap do we bait with this?"

"Good question..."

It took until they'd finished cleaning up the apartment to put together a plan they felt had a hope of working. The groundwork was very basic, and again, nothing he'd not had to do in relation to the seedier aspects of his job with Cox Media.

"Explain what you're doing," Blot said, watching over his shoulder as he opened up his laptop. "I'm here to learn."

He plugged in a headset and slid it on.

"First things first. We need a burner number. Usually, it's because you don't want your number on a spam list, but it's also handy to make sure no one can find their way back to you if things start to go in the direction of libel or slander. There are websites that do it."

"And websites are the things on your computer?"

"Basically."

He entered some bogus information into a switchboard site and earned himself a temporary phone number.

"Okay, next. We need to set up a call with the man himself. We don't have the phone number of Commissioner Magnuson directly, and even if we did, people like that don't answer their own phones. They have people for that."

"Like food tasters in old kingdoms?"

"... I guess? Regardless, if we want to get through to this guy, we need to lob him a softball. Take it from the man behind the camera, if you want to guarantee a politician's PR folks will pass an opportunity to them, make sure it's a photo op for something related to small business."

"Why?"

"Because small businesses are the backbone of our economy. Near as I can figure, that's the first thing politicians learn when they start prepping for on-camera stuff." He slapped down a pad with hastily written notes. "Now you're sure about this stuff?"

"If those words hit the ears of a shade, they'll return the message. And they'll want to talk to me directly."

"Can you even talk on the phone?"

"If we show up to each other on photos, I can't imagine the phone will be any different."

He took a breath. "Okay then, here goes."

Alan punched in the number for Commissioner Magnuson's public relations representative.

"Magnuson campaign headquarters. Bringing law and order in 2018."

"Hello, my name is Killgore Dawn." He flinched at the absurd name, but Blot nodded encouragingly. "I'm the leader of a little informal chamber of commerce called the Shadestrong Committee. We're a small business collective composed of Philadelphia natives, twenty-five merchants strong."

"Well that's great to hear! Candidate Magnuson is a strong believer that small business is the backbone of our economy."

Blot smirked.

"Oh, all of us here know that Mr. Magnuson is the small-business candidate. We know he's been making big promises to help locals like us, and we'd love to invite him to a small-business luncheon, just to say thank you and formally pledge our support."

"I see."

"Yes, we've already got photographers lined up and we've got some of the local news affiliates interested. We'd just love to have the candidate there personally."

"May I ask, who are some of the members of your little collective?"

He glanced at his notes and fired off a veritable yellow pages of wholesome local businesses. Local butchers, hardware stores, drug stores, corner markets, and restaurants. All of them local, all of them real, and all of them closed so that the PR lady couldn't call them to verify.

"... And I'd also like to make it clear that we've got the names and addresses of hundreds of citizens who we feel would be more than willing to contribute to a campaign that supports our businesses. Names and addresses, hundreds of them, from Mr. Dawn."

"Okay, great! Well I'll certainly bring this to Commissioner Magnuson first thing in the morning. You'll be hearing from us bright and early if he's interested, and I think he'll be *quite* interested."

"Fantastic. I look forward to hearing from you." He hung up. "And that's that. All we can do is wait."

"I don't know what to hope for," Blot said. "That it goes off exactly as we planned, or that the whole plan falls through and we get to forget this ever happened."

"Either way, we won't know until morning. I think it's time to call it a night."

Chapter 8

Alan paced silently through a strange gray fog. He was in that glorious, peaceful place between dreams. It was a deep, rich, restful place one never remembers upon waking. The place where the brain truly recovers. What little of his mind that was consciously available to him idly wondered what dreamscape awaited him next.

Gradually, a diminutive figure emerged from the mist. She looked to him expectantly, as though she had been waiting for him.

For the first time in memory, Alan felt himself begin to "wake up" while still very much in this place between dreams. It was fitting that his first moment of full, conscious control of his dream was spent trying to remember the name of such a state.

"Is this... I think... I'm lucid dreaming right now, aren't I?"

"If you mean you are able to decide what to dream about, yes," Blot said.

He looked her over. She'd been a fixture of his dreams since he'd unwittingly become embroiled in her plans, but she'd always looked roughly the same. She was distinctively artificial in her appearance, but at least an artificial attempt at humanity. What she was now was undeniably the same being, yet quite different from any prior appearance.

She was the same height as her shadowy self would suggest, not an inch taller than four foot. She had a petite, pear-shaped body, dressed in humble rags. Rather than feet, her legs seemed to taper down to dainty little points lost in the layer of shifting fog. Her head was larger than seemed proportionately appropriate, and her eyes even more so. They were a magnificent swirl of gray around a tall, narrow pupil. Large, pointed ears put him in mind of a goblin. They rose up from the sides of her head where they flanked her wild, churning black hair. The rest of her facial features were small and pixicish, set into a pale face. A tear in her rags matched where she'd been injured by The Dawn, and white bandages showed through from underneath.

Blot fidgeted a bit under the scrutiny of his eyes and tossed her long scarf over her shoulder.

"Blot," Alan said. "This is you. The real you."

"If there's a real me, this is it," she said. "It's how I looked back home. Not exactly intimidating, is it?"

"Not really." He crouched a bit to look at her eye to eye. "Kind of adorable, though."

She crossed her arms and huffed. "There are only two ways you're ever supposed to see the 'real' shade who has chosen you as a host. Either as another human like you, or as something far too terrifying to trifle with, like the combat form. This?" She spread her arms to present herself. "Is forbidden."

"I guess it wouldn't help bending a human to your whims if they knew you were cute as a button."

"Watch yourself," she said. "I'm baring my soul to you. Don't rub it in."

"What's this all about?"

"If our past adventures are any indication, survival is going to be a skin-of-our-teeth affair, if that. And I wanted to..." She lowered her eyes, and something like a blush came to her cheeks. "I wanted to show you something. Something I think you could appreciate. There might not be another chance. But I'm going to need your help."

"Why? With what?"

"Even though we're linked, we can't share much more than notions between us unless it is mutually agreed upon. This is *your* dream, not mine. So you'll have to sculpt it." She held out her hand. "I promise it'll be quick. And I hope it'll be worth it."

He took her hand. It never dawned on him that he should hesitate. Immediately, their surroundings started to change. A landscape started to reveal itself around them, and it did so in the way that only a dream could. There was no visual indication that things were changing. One moment there was naught but shifting gray fog. The next moment there was a sweeping field, black as pitch, that somehow felt as though it had always been there.

In moments, they were pacing through ankle-deep ashen "snow." A dazzling white sky hung over their heads, streaked with hazy black and speckled with sparkling stars that were like flecks of pepper on a clean white plate.

"I don't know if there is even a name for this place," she said quietly. "From birth, we're mostly fixated on *your* world. I only ever called it 'home.'" She looked up to him. "You don't have to hold my hand anymore."

He didn't realize he'd still been holding it, but he obligingly released it.

"It's... striking. It's like a negative of our world." He looked to her. "Not in the 'worse' sense, in the color-flipped sense. Is it all like this? Sweeping fields?"

"No. No, there are cities. Not like yours. But they are cities."

A few steps later, they were in just such a place. It was bustling and active, but almost impossible for him to make sense of. Roughly cut stone, stacked haphazardly, formed the architecture. Tall, narrow towers jutted precariously into the air, contrasting gorgeously against the white sky. Other shades came and went, mostly visible as white eyes bobbing among the dark corners. The air was thick with odd smells—salty, spicy aromas. Murmured voices filled his ears as he watched creatures like Blot argue and haggle. It was equal parts renaissance fair, goblin kingdom, and Escher lithograph.

"This is what you left behind to come here," he said. "It's really something."

Blot sighed. "I don't even miss it. Like I said, all we ever do is fixate on your world. We wait until our chance to go through and do our duty. Officially, we're doing it to protect our home from you people before you figure out how to come through and wipe us out. But now I don't know."

She crouched and scooped up some of the ashen substance that drifted against walls there in the city. "Now that I've seen your world, I wonder if perhaps it is more about greed. Jealousy. I wonder if the ones in charge just want your world for their own."

She dumped the black stuff from her hand and brushed it clean on her rags. "It wouldn't be the only lie I've been told." She looked up to him, but he was lost in thought. "What's wrong?"

"I'm just curious. This might be a silly question, but how *old* is your world?"

"How old is *any* world? It goes back to the beginning, whenever that was. At least as old as yours. The stories go that we're just a shadow of your world, cast at the same time yours was created. Though, at this point I'd take that with a grain of salt just like everything else I've been told."

"Why is it still so..." He twiddled is fingers. "Middle-ages?"

"What do you mean?"

"We've got cars and planes and electricity. You're still turning hogs on spits."

"That's not a hog, it's a snit. They're very bitter, kind of like coffee."

"You know what I mean."

"You guys *need* those things." She poked him in the ribs. "You're trapped in these meaty shapes and have to build things to get things done. We're a little more malleable and a bit better at getting reality to do our bidding. Though, I suppose focusing ourselves upon seizing your world has kept us from spending much time making our world better."

Blot hopped with a gymnast's nimbleness to the top of a wall that was either half-built or half-collapsed. She reached down to help him climb up after her.

"As near as I can figure," she said, leading him onto a roof and through a window. "You are the first human to see our world, even if it is only a dream of it."

They spiraled their way up the steps, Blot's eyes shifting to pools of featureless white whenever they were entirely in shadow.

"I appreciate you showing it to me, but why?" he asked.

She led him out through a doorway onto a new rooftop. It towered high over the city, far higher than the steps they'd climbed to reach it. A landscape opened below him. Little clusters of cities and villages barely visible against the endless and otherwise featureless black ground.

"I don't know, really. I can never come back here. And I don't really know if I care to. But I just... I wanted to share it with you. I've seen so much of your life, so many new things in so little time. I just wanted to return the favor."

"It's beautiful."

She grinned and plopped down on the tiles of the roof to gaze over it. "That's a polite lie. But I appreciate it."

They sat in silence for a time, gazing over her remembrance of her homeland. Then the very fabric of the place started to quiver as a tone danced at the edge of hearing.

"What's that?"

"The computer is ringing. It's the call. Wake up!"

Alan bolted upright and dragged himself from bed, eyes bleary. It was still night. He didn't take the time to figure out what time it was. There was no telling how many times the computer's simulated phone had rung.

He slapped the headset on his head and mashed the space bar. "Hello," he said, wiping his eyes with the back of his hand.

"Killgore Dawn?" said a calm, measured voice on the other end of the call.

"Who?" he replied sluggishly.

Blot slapped him on the back of the head.

"Oh, yes, right! Dawn speaking. Sorry. You woke me up."

"This is Magnuson. Contrary to the recommendations of my PR team, I thought it might be worth giving you a call directly."

"Contrary to recommendation? I thought for sure they'd be all over an opportunity to show your support for local business."

"There's no Killgore Dawn in local business," he said. "A few Dawn Killgores scattered through the country, but no Killgore Dawn."

"I'm... new."

"I'd wager the only thing new about you is your shade. And I'll have a word with him."

He cleared his throat. "Her, actually."

"Put her on."

Alan looked to Blot. He removed his headset and held it out. Her shadowy hand took it and drew it into the shadows with her. While she put it on, Alan tried to ignore the way the wire just vanished into the wall. He switched the audio to the speakers so they could both listen in on the call.

"I'm here," she said.

"One moment," said Magnuson.

The next voice to speak sounded like it was the sort of thing that would echo up a drainpipe with warnings about what would happen if one slept without first saying their prayers.

"Which one are you?" it said.

"I'm Blot."

"The same Blot who attacked Dun?" it rumbled.

"I had some difficulty getting my host to see the value of our way of thinking. But we've had some run-ins with The Dawn since then and he's come around," she said. "Who are you?"

"Ruck."

Blot shuddered. "It is an honor to speak to you, Ruck. I grew up on stories of your prowess."

"You have something for me?" he said.

"Yes. Yes, as a matter of fact, our run-in with The Dawn has provided us with quite a windfall. I have the names, phone numbers, and addresses of a great many of their members. We were able to steal a phone from one of them."

"You faced The Dawn and survived?" he said doubtfully.

"We are wily."

"Give me the names."

"I want to meet face-to-face to hand them over."

"You don't need to meet to give us the names. Give them now."

She shut her eyes and tried to summon up some authority. "My host is a loser, Ruck. There's precious little we can do with him as he is." She opened her eyes and glanced at him apologetically. "We can help, but we need to be part of the fold. I want to meet with you personally so we can find a place for him and start working immediately."

"No."

"Then you won't get the names."

"You would deny aid to the cause of your own kind?"

"What exactly are *you* doing by leaving me to try to build my host up on my own?" she snapped.

"Until Magnuson wins the election, we must take great care."

"All the more reason to have someone aboard who not only has got the names of The Dawn and where they operate out of but also has survived multiple clashes with them without the benefit of armed guards from the local population."

Ruck did not reply immediately. The only sound for a few moments was a distant murmur and the odd creaking sound of a handset being held too tightly.

"Very well... You will meet with us. We will hire your host. You will provide us all of your information and the means you used to escape the members of The Dawn you faced."

"Good. I'm sure I'll be of help."

Blot jabbed a nearby pad of paper. Alan grabbed a pen and carefully transcribed the address.

"Head here immediately. The sooner we know the place of our enemies, the sooner we can strike them down."

"As you wish, Ruck. It will be an honor to serve with you."

Alan hung up the phone. Blot relaxed. The headset popped out of the wall. She released a sigh of relief.

"It's a lot easier to be brave over the phone," she observed.

"You should try emails and texts," he said. "You seemed nervous about the name Ruck."

"He's a soldier. One of our best. One of the personal guards to Stigma, our leader. I'm not keen on our prospects if Dun tells him to take us out."

"If Dun tells him to?"

"Yes. He's a soldier. He'll follow orders."

"So he's a henchman?" Alan said.

"He's a little more than a henchman," she said.

"What I mean is he's a fighter rather than a thinker?"

"That's fair."

"And he's paired up with the would-be senator, taking orders from the shade paired up with an intern?"

"I've explained this already. We didn't exactly have a lot of time and insight when we showed up."

He shook his head. "This is weird. But I guess not half as weird as everything else that's going on." He stood. "Let's get ready. With any luck, we'll be able to get everything we need and have this whole mission behind us by sunrise." He started to gather some things. "Uh... Out of curiosity, when you say this guy is a soldier, does that mean he's just really good at the whole combat-form thing?"

"I'd rather not fill your head with thoughts of what he can do. Let's just say we'll both be better off if we don't get a demonstration of his abilities."

"I see. Well, that has done the opposite of set my mind at ease, so we're already off to a great start..."

Alan huddled a little tighter in his coat as he hurried along the street. He'd parked his car six blocks away from the address. Ideally, that would be far enough away that if things went horribly wrong and the police got involved too soon, it would be outside their circle of scrutiny.

"I'm getting dizzy," Blot said, sliding by as he passed under another streetlight.

"Sorry about that," Alan said.

"If we live through this, can we at least find a way to keep your car a little darker?"

"Sure, yeah. They do window tinting. And it'd be really nice if you could stop prefacing every statement with 'if we live through this.'"

"Yes. That *would* be nice."

He raised his eyes to the building ahead. "This is the place."

The address they'd been given was of a taller-than-average office building near the center of town. It was one of those places that held the offices of a dozen or so businesses, though predawn as it was, he very much suspected the only people in the place right now were those in on the meeting. He was quite certain he recognized the commissioner's personal car from some of the photos floating around Cox Media over the course of the election. That said, there was no shortage of cars in the surrounding parking lot. Certainly more than would be necessary for the two shades they already knew about.

"I really wish you would have brought a weapon. You people have some really great weapons."

"I don't think I could bring myself to use a weapon."

"I'd be happy to."

"I know. That's why I didn't give you one either. Are you okay carrying the rest of the stuff?"

"No problem. Carrying stuff is easy."

Alan approached the service entrance as instructed. A brutish-looking man stood guard. He was unlike the off-duty/retired police officers that had served as Magnuson's security escort back at the warehouse meeting. These men were a bit more brash and obvious about the presence of weaponry and the willingness to use it.

"Against the wall," the man instructed.

"I'm here on the invitation of—"

A ham-sized fist slapped him in the chest and thumped him into the wall. "I don't ask twice."

Alan endured one of the rougher and more thorough security pat-downs of his life, reinforcing his decision not to arm himself. A few things became clear during the search. First, this man at the very least wasn't a host. The fact that his shadow was very clearly his own was a good indication, but also the fact that in all of his searching he'd not made any attempt to address Blot.

"You're good. Inside. Service elevator. Third floor."

Alan nodded stiffly and hurried along through minimally lit hallways.

"This is more like it," Blot said, sliding up along the wall to travel beside him. "This is the sort of environment a shade thrives in."

"Yeah." He glanced over his shoulder. "Did you get a criminal vibe from that guy at the door?"

"He didn't seem very mannerly. Should I start the thing now?"

"Yeah, I think so. It's the big button on the left side."

"I know, I know. We rehearsed, remember? And hush, there's another guard."

Sure enough, a larger, more solid version of the man at the door awaited him at the elevator.

"Against the wall," the man-mountain instructed.

"But the guy at the door just—"

Again, he was slammed against the wall and frisked with all the gentleness of a mugging.

"I'm starting to detect a pattern," Blot said.

Two floors and a third frisking later, Alan was shoved through a door into a dim room. The door clicked behind him. He turned to find the room set up like something out of a secret-society induction ceremony. Six figures sat in a half circle around a single chair in the center of the room.

"Blot... I am not certain if I should be frustrated or gratified that you've maneuvered yourself into a useful position again," uttered Dun from the darkness.

"I thought this was supposed to just be—" Alan began.

"This doesn't concern you," Dun said. "Speak when spoken to."

"Uh... yes, sir."

"Blot, you have the names?" Dun said.

"I do." She slid forward and extended a hand.

With a magician's flourish, her cunning little hand produced an index card. It flipped out into being, hanging in the air before Alan. Dun reached for it, his hand sliding along the ground to take its shadow from Blot's. Alan had a bit of difficulty following what was happening, as the two individuals performing the transaction were long projections on the floor, but the card was directly in front of him.

"This is a single address," Dun said. "You said you had hundreds."

"And you tried to kill me last time we met. Forgive my caution, but I don't intend to turn over *all* of the information until I'm sure you're not going to try to get rid of me once you have what you want."

Dun squinted his eyes. "Sensible." He flipped up the card and glanced over it. After reading the information, he shifted aside a bit and held out the card. "Commissioner, if you would?"

The half-visible figure of Magnuson took the card. He fetched his phone. The glow of his screen as he dialed the number confirmed it was indeed the candidate.

"Lieutenant Martinez?" he said. "Yeah. It's Magnuson. Are you alone, like I asked? Good. I've got an address here. Run it for me. Let me know if there's been anything suspicious there in the last few days."

"What are you doing?" Blot asked.

"In a way, we are checking to see just how wily you really are. If you are smart, you'll have given us an address that we can be certain is associated with The Dawn."

"Ah. Well, I think you'll be satisfied." She surveyed the rest of the group. "I didn't realize so many of us got as far south as Philadelphia. Of course I recognize you and Ruck. I do not know the other four."

"Lag is another of my students. She has found her way to Alicia Coke. A fine selection, might I add. Rather well placed in the criminal underworld. Ms. Coke is responsible for the security here today. Beside her is Crum, who has selected a banker. That should prove quite useful. Shem and Sham are subordinates of Ruck's. Midlevel soldiers, shifter focused. They've selected a brother and sister of little consequence. A grocer and something called an Uber driver. They make for useful, unassuming go-betweens. Frankly, the soon-to-be senator and the criminal should serve all of our requirements quite ably. So you will understand if I doubt the value of you, an underpowered and demonstrably untrustworthy shade and her... *photographer* was it?"

Magnuson hung up and turned to the others.

"There were reports of a disturbance at the provided address. When officers arrived, the place was recently cleared out, but they did turn up some booklets containing coded language and imagery consistent with The Dawn," he said.

"For one, we've just proved we were in contact with The Dawn as we said. That's where they held us for questioning. We escaped." Blot gestured at the smaller but still very present hole in her silhouette. "But not without a price."

"And as I faced no additional pressure from them, I presume they failed to get anything out of you."

"That's right," Blot said.

"Very well. You are potentially a worthwhile soldier."

"Potentially worthwhile?" said Alicia Coke. "If she's got even a handful of names from The Dawn, I'll get my boys out there to wipe them out."

"You should let the cops take care of things," Magnuson said.

"The cops can't take care of things unless they kill a few of us first. How about you just make sure the cops don't get in my way while I do the dirty business, Commissioner?"

"I'm confident I can have these men hauled in on suspicion. We can assign a likely charge later."

"Enough, both of you," Dun ordered. "We'll discuss such matters later. The issue at hand remains Blot and whether she deserves to be included in our operations. Provided the rest of the names and addresses are more fruitful than the example, this is indeed a valuable addition to our cause. But what of your host? What good will he do us?"

"He's a fine photographer," Blot said.

"So not any more useful than Shem's and Sham's hosts."

"If I may?" Alan said, feeling oddly as though he was in a particularly intense job interview.

Dun looked at him wearily. "Speak."

"Blot can vouch that I have a number of skills useful in surveillance. I also have connections within the police force—"

"Those are handled far more capably by Magnuson."

"And I have connections within the media."

"The media." Dun narrowed his eyes. "Yes. That has proved to be of rather greater consequence than I had anticipated. Not without value. I believe we can overlook your prior indiscretions if you can pass one final test."

"I am sure I am equal to the challenge," Blot said.

"We shall see. Ruck."

The sizable shadow linked to Magnuson approached.

"Search her," Dun instructed.

Ruck lashed a shadowy hand toward Blot, scaling up as he did. The hand wrapped entirely around her head, reducing any complaints she might have had to muffled cries.

"Whoa! Hey," Alan said. "The goons along the way searched me already."

"Yes. They searched you. They didn't search Blot."

Ruck shook her violently. One by one, items started to slide from the shadows and rattle to the ground: A cell phone, a wad of cash, a handful of change, a large flashlight... and a small, blinking electronic gadget.

Blot's hands clutched madly at a final object as Dun snatched up the unidentified gadget.

"Stop. What is this..."

"That's a recorder!" Magnuson said.

"She was wearing a wire!" shouted Coke.

"You deceitful little... what else does she have?" Dun demanded.

Ruck wrestled with her, trying to strip away the final bulky object she gripped. She had no hope of overpowering him, but she managed to tear herself away from his grip long enough to heave the object behind her. It snapped out of the shadows and lofted toward Alan. He caught it and held it up. It was his camera, with a downright monstrous flash attached.

He pressed the shutter release. From the effect it had on the rest of the room, one would have thought he'd thrown a grenade. All six shades launched toward the back wall. As only Alan was behind the flash, only Blot was spared the worst of the sudden, intense light. Even the humans in the room were briefly dazzled by the blinding flash.

"So, photographers are useless, are we?" Alan jabbed.

Blot snatched up the phone, the recorder, and the flashlight. She huddled behind him.

"Just run, Alan!"

Alan kicked the door to the meeting room open and dashed into the hallway.

The man standing guard got as far as raising his weapon and shouting a warning before Blot slid up to his shadow and yanked the gun out of his hand.

"What the hell?!" the man yelped.

"Ha *ha!*" Blot proclaimed.

She pulled the trigger. Three things happened in rapid succession. The shot missed by a mile. More troubling was the muzzle flash. It sent Blot jerking backward, which, combined with the recoil, sent the gun whistling past Alan's head to clatter along the ground.

Alan, only slightly more prepared for the supernatural happenings than the guard, managed to send him sprawling with a frantic shoulder block and dashed down the hallway.

"The stairs!" Alan said, sprinting for the glowing exit sign. "They'll probably be able to shut down the elevator and we'll be trapped!"

Behind them, he could hear the other hosts and shades rushing from the doorway. Blot tossed him the flashlight, which he shined behind him as he ran. With the other hand, he did his best to dial the police while still moving at full speed. As it turned out, even emergency calls required a bit more coordination than he could spare, so he abandoned the call and focused on getting away.

He burst out into the stairwell and briefly considered finding a way to bar the door. To his dismay, though not his shock, there weren't any handy objects to lock people out of the emergency evacuation route. Voices and flashlights below suggested the thugs from the first floor had been summoned by the gunfire.

"Crap, crap, crap!" Alan cried. Since down was no longer an option, he bounded up the stairs.

"Where are you going?" Blot cried. "We'll bash our way through the thugs!"

"You've got a hole through your chest and barely a few hours to recover."

"I have enough oomph to clock a couple of thugs!"

A stuttering burst of bullets peppered the steps below them.

"Oh! Guns. I forgot they would *all* have guns," she said.

Alan was in no state to respond. His tried-and-true plan of running and hiding was already well underway. He bounded up steps three at a time, rocketing past three landings before choosing a floor to duck inside. He found himself on floor six, which seemed to be a call center. Predawn as it was, it was empty. The floor was divided up into hundreds of cubicles. He dropped down and crawled through the aisles until he found one to huddle into.

"Well," he gasped, cowering under a desk. "They've got a whole building to search. We should be safe if we lie low."

Blot slid down into the darkness beside him, having resumed her normal form. "Did we do enough?"

"I'm not sure... Dun did most of the talking, so I'm not sure about the recording, but I'm pretty sure we caught that bit where the commish and the crime boss were busy trying to work out whether to kill or frame a bunch of people. That's something, at least."

"It's not *much* more than we already had," Blot said.

"I know..." He pulled up his camera and flicked through the photos he'd shot. "It's one of the lousiest pictures I've ever taken, but I've got Magnuson and Coke in the same shot. That'll raise some questions, at least. But only if we survive."

Alan pulled out his phone and dialed the police.

"911. Please state your emergency!"

"I'm in 212 Second Street. There are multiple men with guns. I need help!"

"Okay, sir. Let me just... could you repeat the address, sir?"

"212 Second."

"I am transferring you to a specialist dispatcher. Please hold."

"Please hold?! But—"

There were a sequence of clicks, and a new voice answered. "Sir, you say there are multiple gunmen?"

"Yes! Send help!"

"I suggest you stay right where you are, sir. And stay on the line."

He sank a little lower and listened closely to the 911 dispatcher. He'd only ever called 911 a handful of times. Most of them in just the last few days. This was the first time he'd been in such genuine distress when he did so. But somehow, he would have expected a little more urgency.

"Sir?"

"Yeah! Yeah, I'm here," he whispered.

"What floor are you on, sir?"

"One of the upper floors."

"What floor exactly, sir?"

"All of the gunmen are below me, so—"

"I need to know what floor you are on, sir."

Alan narrowed his eyes. "Your name wouldn't happen to be Martinez, would it?"

"Tell me what floor you are on, sir."

He hung up.

"What now?" Blot asked.

"Plan B."

He scrolled up to another contact. After a few rings, a sluggish voice answered. "Hullo..."

"Jessie! It's Alan. I'm in trouble."

"Alan? What's going on?"

"Remember when I asked about finding a way to get those people in that video locked up?"

"Yeah?"

"Well, things have gotten out of control."

"Why are you calling me? Call the station!"

"One of the people here's the commissioner. I'm pretty sure 911 just tried to get me to rat myself out."

"... Alan, that doesn't make any sense."

"Do you have any idea how much of the crap I've seen and done in the last three days makes no sense?"

"Look, I'm home. And I'm not one of the brass. I can't just dispatch a squad car."

"What should I do?"

"Where are you?"

"212 Second Street."

"What kind of building is it?"

"It's an office building."

Distantly, a door opened.

"Hurry!" he whispered.

"The fire alarm. Pull it. I'll see if I can get a call in. I might be able to get it elevated."

"Right. Right. Great idea. If you hear from me again, it's because you saved my life." He hung up.

"They're coming, Alan. What do we do?" Blot asked.

"We've got to set off the fire alarm."

"How?"

"Find an alarm box, get those sprinklers to go off, or—"

"I can do that!"

"No, wait!" he hissed.

Blot stretched up and swiped her hand out of the shadows. The quick blow was enough to dislodge the sprinkler head. All the other sprinklers sprang to life, along with a blaring fire alarm.

"I did it!" she crowed.

"I would have waited until we were on another floor..." Alan said, trying to shield the camera from the water.

The thugs investigating the floor shouted orders to each other. Water poured down. He slithered low along the floor.

"Where are they?" he said. "I can't see them or hear them."

She slid herself farther along the floor. "Back, back. The other way," she urged.

Row by row, Alan sloshed his way as quietly as possible while Blot directed him. Two more thugs showed up, but even with four sets of eyes, a whole floor of an office building was an awful lot of space to search. With the falling water to cover the sound of Alan's motion and Blot to direct him, he managed to slip out at another staircase. Plenty of angry, shouted orders made it clear that heading down was still not an option, so he crept up a few more levels and ducked inside.

Alan, huddled under a new desk, spoke quietly into a phone.

"Yeah, Mr. Cox. I know you were asleep. And I know you fired me. But I'm just saying something is going down and you're going to want people here. Check the police scanner, do what you've got to do. I'm telling the truth, and one way or another, this is going to be a big story. ... Yeah... Yeah, good. And I promise you the exclusive."

He hung up and leaned out the door of a very middle-management office he'd ducked into on a fresh floor a few more flights up. It was outside the block of floors currently pouring water.

"Okay. Okay," he breathed. "We stopped leaving soggy footprints and I hear sirens. We'll just lie low and wait. We only have to make it a few minutes before the cops chase everyone off." He paused. "Unless that's just the fire truck."

"I don't like that we're hiding *in* the building, Alan."

"I don't like it either, but since every way out of the building has guys with guns, this is what we've got. Let's just..."

He was interrupted by two doors swinging open violently. Alan ducked back into the room and flattened himself against the wall. The distant snuffle of animal snouts could be heard.

"What the hell? Do they have hounds or something?" he whispered urgently.

"Uh oh..."

He squinted at her. "Uh oh what?"

"It's... probably nothing..."

"It's not going to be nothing. At this point, it's *never* going to be nothing again."

Blot shrank down a bit. "There were two shades down there with shifter training."

"You mentioned that sort of thing to me before. What exactly can I expect?"

Blot hesitated.

"I need to know what we're dealing with. What kind of shape?" he said warily. "We're not talking werewolves, are we?"

"No, no, no." She cleared her throat. "More likely a were-snit."

The flimsy wall rattled behind him. He scrambled to the center of the room.

"Are we talking claws and teeth?" he said, brandishing his camera.

"Yes. But also snouts. The better for tracking."

The door rattled. Alan flicked the switch to start charging his monster flash again, but it released a worrisome pop followed by an acrid electronic sizzle.

"Weather-proof my ass..." he muttered.

Blot started to draw herself up into her combat form. She was shaky, but at least large enough to match Adam.

"The flash wouldn't do any good for these anyway. The human itself is the threat," she said. "Be ready to run."

He popped off the broken flash and stuffed it into his jacket pocket. As far as he could tell, the built-in flash was still good, and he still had the flashlight. The door rattled harder. He raised the camera.

"I told you a flash won't work."

"I know. But whatever it is, you better believe I'm going to want a picture."

Finally, the door buckled and fell forward. Alan reflexively snapped a picture before his brain even registered what had bashed the door down.

It was just as well. Had he waited, he might not have had the fortitude to do so.

A pair of beasts stared him down. As Blot promised, they certainly weren't werewolves. For one, they weren't furry, or at least, not furrier than a normal human. They were broadly canine in posture, though with elongated snouts and long greyhound-like limbs. Their clothes were mostly intact, the limbs simply extending out of the garments' legs and arms, and baring a long, sunken abdomen. They'd not gained any mass. The influence simply reshaped what they had into something spindly and feral.

Blot took full advantage of their less-than-imposing mass. With a backhand of her twisted form, she knocked them aside. Alan sprinted through the cleared doorway and dashed toward the door.

They scrabbled to their feet and gave chase. The humans-turned-beasts were fast. Long limbs took them up to terrifying speed in just a few strides. When Alan turned a corner and dashed down a hallway, the one directly on his tail tumbled and slid across the floor in a tangle of ungainly legs. A stride later the second slammed into the first.

While they were trying to untangle themselves. Alan skidded out into the main hallway and dashed for the stairs.

"You can't do that to *me*, can you?" he yelped.

"Not without a few months of practice and a lot of trial and error."

He reached the stairs and turned back in time to see them slide into view and smash into the far wall.

"Thank god they're not graceful."

"Would *you* be if you suddenly had different limbs?"

"I genuinely hope I never find out."

He shoved his way out into the stairwell and made it a half-flight down when the first bullets started flying and chased him back up.

"You can't keep climbing. Up is not the way out!" Blot said.

Alan didn't reply. This was not a time for logic. This was a time for running away from bullets.

Angry, confused shouts echoed up and down the stairwell. The twisted hosts of Shem and Sham tumbled out and nearly went sprawling down the stairs. Below, heavies with guns first took aim, then holstered their weapons as Coke shouted orders. Alan left them all behind. He didn't even bother trying another floor. His mind commanded him to go up, and up is where he went.

Not until he spilled out of an emergency exit on the roof did Alan get enough of his wits together to realize this was quite possibly the last place he should have been heading. There wasn't even a second door leading back down. He was cornered.

The faint rosy glow of dawn was just beginning to paint the sky to the east. On the street below, two different types of sirens rang out. He inched toward the edge of the roof to find a fire truck had pulled up along with two cop cars. A distant sputtering thrum signaled the approach of a helicopter with a local news affiliate painted on the side.

"I guess you place enough phone calls to enough places and people start to listen," Alan said.

He peered down along the side of the building, hoping perhaps to find a fire escape, but they were far too high up for that. What he found instead was that the parking lot formerly filled with the cars of the little enclave now seemed a bit emptier. Most notably, the car Alan had surmised belonged to the commissioner. He'd almost certainly gotten away moments after things started to fall to pieces.

"Blot!" barked a voice from the doorway.

Alan and Blot turned. Dun and Lenny had emerged from the emergency doors. The twisted—and now battered—forms of Shem and Sham's hosts lingered in the doorway behind. Lenny shakily held a gun.

"I was right to consider you two a liability," Dun rumbled. "You are fools who have achieved only one useful act." He rose up out of the shadows and extended a spindly claw. "Give me the names of The Dawn. Let your pointless lives serve one purpose."

Alan took a step back. "It won't do you any good. You don't know the code to get into the phone."

"Then tell me the code."

"Never."

The helicopter drew nearer. Alan raised his arm to obscure his face.

"Blot, remember your allegiance," Dun barked.

She rose up between Dun and Alan, visibly fatigued, but defiant.

"You tried to kill me. My only allegiance is to myself and to Alan."

"They you shall *die*."

The shades launched toward each other. Alan clicked on the flashlight. It hit Dun like a firehose, forcing him back. Blot was swept aside. But inch by inch, Dun fought forward against the light. Blot wasn't kidding when she said the others were stronger than her. If he was going to immobilize this shade, he'd need something more powerful.

As if it were an answer to his desperate hopes for salvation, the news-copter clicked on its spotlight. The beam was powerful enough to flatten both Dun and Blot against the roof. The twisted creatures in the doorway fled back into the bowels of the building.

"Lenny! Kill him!" Dun ordered.

The intern shakily held the gun. "I... I don't know if I can do that..." Lenny said.

"Do as I say!"

"You never said anything about me having to pull any triggers. And there's a camera."

"Do as I say or you will *suffer*..."

The helicopter circled them, causing the shadows to shift. Alan backed away, pressing himself to the railing as Blot rotated around and started to slide toward the edge beside him. He looked back. The spotlight was projecting the shadow of the building onto the side of the next building.

"I think... I think I have an idea..." Alan murmured.

"Good. Because we need one," Blot said.

She was starting to vanish over the edge under the influence of the circling spot. This also brought Dun creeping closer to him.

"I think I'm going to need a hug," he said.

"... That might not be a good idea," Blot said, now creeping up along the far building.

"Do you have a better one?" he said.

"Lenny, kill this man!" Dun ordered.

The intern shakily took closer aim.

Alan took a deep breath. He leaned back. "Now!" he cried.

A dark arm snapped up out of the shadows and drew tight against his chest. The icy grip of the shadows swept over his body. For a moment, he could feel himself stretched across hundreds of feet. He looked up. Blot's shadowy form had held tight to the fire escape halfway down the building across the street. She snapped toward it and let herself slide a few flights down along the side of the building before breathlessly releasing him.

He tumbled a few terrifying inches and clattered onto the cold metal grating of a fire-escape landing.

They were in the shadow of the building, and watched as the flailing, lashing form of Dun glided across the building above them. Faint claw marks crackled across the bricks, but Alan had timed the escape properly. Dun wasn't lined up with the fire escape. If he were to attempt the same stunt, Lenny would be left clinging to the side of the building. Or more likely, plummeting to the street below.

Alan placed his hand over his heart and pulled himself shakily to his feet. From the reaction of the law enforcement in the street below, the general consensus was that whoever had just vanished from the roof had fallen over the edge. Though they wouldn't be able to find the body, chances were very good no one would suggest he'd flitted across the street in the embrace of a sentient shadow.

He raised his camera and snapped a few final pictures. "Okay, Blot," he said, handing over the camera for her to tote. "Let's get out of here. I think I owe you an espresso."

"What's an espresso?"

"You're gonna love it."

Epilogue

L unchtime the following day—just a few hours later, in fact—Alan found himself in Mr. Cox's office once more. The media magnate stared him up and down as they each slumped into their seats.

"You look like you've been through hell, Fontaine."

"I may have visited parts of it," he said.

In truth, it was an apt observation. Despite a shower, the frazzled, stretched-to-the-limit look had yet to leave Alan's face. He had two fat bruises on his head, one of which was now creeping down to form a nice black eye. Little gouges near the hairline had yet to fully heal. His eyes were sunken and dark from lack of sleep.

"Care to tell me how you knew something would be going down in that building?"

"Let's just say I've got some sources that like to lurk in some shady corners," he said.

"Well, thanks to you, I was able to get Marie-Anna out to get some shots."

"So early in the morning, while you were in bed. I'm surprised you were able to reach her," Alan said.

"He probably didn't have to reach far," Blot jabbed.

Alan snickered.

"What's funny?" Cox said.

"Nothing. Nothing."

The red-faced man gave him a bit more of a sideways glance.

"You being so well informed, and you having demanded this meeting, something tells me you've got some shots of your own."

Alan reached into his pocket and held out a memory card. Cox snatched it and dumped the contents onto his computer. It didn't take long. There were only a few photos and a short snippet of audio. His former boss brought up previews.

"... Is that..." He pointed. "That's Magnuson. Looking like a deer in the headlights. And who's this?"

"Alicia Coke."

Cox typed in the name. "Alicia Coke, under investigation from the Organized Crimes Division for multiple counts of this, that, and the other? Alicia Coke, the one who got hauled in this morning for questioning after attempting to escape an armed incident at a Philadelphia commercial structure?"

"That's the one."

"What were they doing in the same place at the same time?"

"Listen to the audio."

Cox double-clicked it and was treated to a brief snippet, just a few seconds long, of them discussing framing someone.

"There's got to be more," he said.

"I'm sure there is. But that's plenty for an exclusive, wouldn't you say?"

"From an anonymous source, I assume?"

"Ideally."

Cox nodded. "Yeah. That'll get clicks all right." He pulled out his check-book. "The contracted price is—" he began.

"You terminated my contract," Alan said.

Cox gave him a hard glance. "This is going to cost me, isn't it?"

"There's going to be some negotiation, yes. Starting with you giving me a little more consideration come assignment time," Alan said. "Assuming you want me back in the pool."

"Is there going to be more stuff like this?"

"I don't think I'm going to be able to avoid it. The shadow operative who helped me with this is here to stay."

"Then you're damn well back in the freelance rotation," he said, scrawling an extra zero on the check.

After depositing the check, Alan found himself a nice, quiet booth at the diner for a celebratory patty melt. It was the first moment in days that he felt as though there was a chance to breathe. He put that breath to the most important use he could think of.

"Yeah, Mom. No, I'm fine. I just wanted to..."

He glanced up. A TV over the breakfast counter silently played through the news of they day. Cox had worked quickly. Already the photo was circulating. Footage of Magnuson shielding his face and rigidly refusing comment was front and center.

"Are you near a TV? Turn on ABC."

"Just a second," she said. "Okay. I've got it on."

"You see the pictures they're showing?"

"Not very good."

"It might not be very good, but it was worth a couple thousand bucks."

"You took that!"

"I sure did."

"I've got to call Deloris and—"

"No, no. Probably best not to spread it around. You'll note it says 'anonymous source.'"

"Oh. Just what have you been up to?" she said warily.

"Don't worry about me. I just wanted to let you know my money problems are over, for a while. How about you? I can afford to send you some money now."

"No, no, you don't have to do that. Once the money comes in from the land sale, I'm sure we'll be fine."

"How long, do you figure?"

"I don't know. They lawyers are still arguing about something."

"I thought it was a done deal."

"You know lawyers..."

"Well let me know if you need anything. I'll talk to you later."

"You too. And congratulations! Pictures on the news and everything!"

He laughed. "Thanks, Mom." He hung up and looked back to the TV. "It wasn't exactly what I'd hoped for," Alan murmured, slapping some ketchup from a bottle.

"You can't always get what you want," Blot said. "But at the very least, he's not going to be a senator."

"Yeah. And I've got to assume at least a few of those people were locked up. I'll have to buy a paper or something and see. That should make it tricky for The Dawn to do them in."

"That is something of an underestimation," muttered a wizened voice.

Alan turned. An old man with a silver-tipped cane hobbled past him and sat stiffly in the booth opposite him. Blot scrambled back and huddled behind Alan.

"You..." Alan said. "How did you find me?"

"You stole a wallet from one of my men. You still have it on you."

Alan felt his pocket, then dug out the purloined item.

"May I?" the old man said, holding out his hand.

Alan handed it over. The man flipped the wallet open. Buried among the credit cards and receipts stuffed inside was a small silver coin. He pulled it out.

"Each of our troops carries one. As easy to find as the dagger."

"So you've been able to follow me the entire time?" Alan said.

"We could. Things were a little frantic or we'd probably have found and killed you ASAP, but you getting his phone..." His eyes narrowed behind his spectacles. "And you having that *friend* of yours, we figured that if we didn't batten down the hatches, we'd be looking at a massacre."

He pocketed the wallet. "But it didn't happen. Not one door got knocked on. Funny, that."

"I don't want anyone killed," Alan said. "Not your side, not my side."

"Mmm... Spoken like a man that doesn't know the stakes. And doesn't quite understand which side is his. But I'll give you this: I wasn't shy about making it clear what I had in store for you, and you spared the lot of us anyway. Old age tends to make a man stubborn. But set in my ways

223

as I might be, I've got to acknowledge that you're not the kind of host I've come to expect. Could be you're not the awful sort. Could be you're playing it a few steps further ahead than we're used to. But a good turn deserves a good turn."

He held out his hand. "Call it a truce."

Alan eyed the offered hand warily. "What are the terms?"

"The terms are we keep an eye on you but we don't put a dagger in you. The Dawn's stretched thin enough; we won't mind having one less shade to worry about. Having one willing to go against the rest could be a help."

"What do we have to do?"

"Keep your nose clean and keep it out of our business."

Alan considered it.

"Arm's getting tired, boy," the old man said.

"What do you think?" Alan said under this breath.

"Do it. But if he tries to stab me again, I'm going to tear his arm off."

Alan shook his hand. "I assume you'll want the phone back?"

"Presumably you've gotten all the information off it already," he said.

"Sure, but it's a hassle to have to replace a phone." Alan produced the stolen device and placed it on the table.

The old man shook his head and pocketed it, then hauled himself to his feet. "You're a strange one, boy." He stole a fry. "Remember the deal. Head down, nose clean, and we'll busy ourselves elsewhere."

He hobbled off, leaving Alan to his meal.

"That's... wow," Blot said.

"What?"

"A truce... They teach of other times the way between worlds has opened and we have come to this place. Never, *never*, did they speak of a truce."

"You'd think that would be the way it would have to end."

"No, *you'd* think that. We'd think it would have to end in annihilation or control. And it's always ended in our side being wiped away. But now there's a truce."

"Between exactly one shade and the cult trying to wipe them out."

"And it's *me*," Blot said. "No... It's *us*."

"How's that make you feel?"

"I don't know. I should hate it. I should feel terrible. Wretched. I should feel like a traitor. And I sort of do. ... But I sort of don't. *We* did this. It's... it's historic. And *we* did it."

"It's an important step. But it's just one step."

"It's a step that no one has ever taken!" Blot said. "Not Stigma, not Dun, not Ruck. No one. And then there's *you*."

"What *about* me?"

"You're calling the shots with that Cox guy. Negotiating your own deal. And why? Because you went and tried to confound some folks, to trick them, to trap them. Your life is better now because of tricks *I* taught you."

"I'm not sure you should be *so* proud of persuading me to do shady... to do unscrupulous things."

"It made your life better, which means it made *us* stronger. And we're going to need that. Because this isn't over, is it? Not nearly."

"Yeah... Just because we've got a truce with The Dawn doesn't mean the shades aren't going to try to get even. And then there's..." Alan looked pensively at his patty melt.

"What are you thinking?" Blot asked.

"I'm thinking there's one more loose end that needs tying up." He reached into his pocket and retrieved the silver bell.

"Oh..." Blot said.

"We've got to do it, don't we? To know where we stand?"

"The only place I want to stand is far away from them. But do what you have to do."

He gave the bell a ring. It barely tinkled before a delicate hand closed around it.

"That won't be necessary, Mr. Fontaine."

He looked up to find both the white-suited individuals standing at the table. He'd not heard or seen them arrive, and no one else in the diner seemed particularly bothered by their sudden appearance.

Dina plucked the bell from his hand.

"You need not ring that bell any longer. We'll be keeping an eye on you from now on," Gabriel said.

"If you get involved in something that warrants our attention, I assure you, we will be well aware," Dina said.

"Is that a good thing or a bad thing?" Alan said. "Are the referees going to throw a red flag?"

"That would be a yellow flag," Gabriel said. "Or a red card, if soccer is your game."

"Sorry. I'm more of a basketball guy," Alan said.

"You needn't mix your metaphors. There are no such things in this particular game," Dina said.

"Violations are not tolerated," Gabriel said.

"Which should give you some indication of our current opinion of your little... alliance."

"Because I'd be dead if you didn't approve. Is that what you're saying?"

"Please," Dina said. "That is a terrible, and telling, assumption you've made."

Alan heaved a breath and tightened his jaw. "Look, could you stop being so vague? The shades are pretty clear about wanting me dead. The Dawn laid it all out, plain and simple. Why do you have to be so spooky. *God!*"

"Listen!" Dina demanded.

The diner fell into silence. Every patron, every employee, even the people on the street outside stopped in place. Waiting. Alan couldn't move. Eyes wide, muscles rigid.

"What we seek is balance," Gabriel said. "What we had before you was balance. Shades and The Dawn, chasing the tails of one another. Each of them both hunters and quarry."

"Predators and prey," Dina said.

"A brief struggle, subtle enough to be ignored by the populace, but substantial enough to be renewed when the time comes," Gabriel said.

"A shade does not oppose a shade," Dina said.

"Not successfully, at any rate," Gabriel said.

"We are inclined to take corrective action."

"It will simply make things flow more smoothly."

"But there are those with far greater influence than us who have taken an interest."

"They have decided that more observation is called for."

Dina leaned forward. "You have the mixed blessing of being interesting, Alan."

"We'll meet again," Gabriel said.

"And until then, please. Do keep our little meetings to yourself," Dina said.

"There is such a thing as professional courtesy," Gabriel agreed.

They paced from the diner, and activity slowly resumed. If anyone else was aware anything had happened, there was no indication. The last to recover was Alan himself. He blinked his burning eyes and shook his head.

"Are you satisfied?" Blot said, a tremble in her voice.

"I got no answers. I'm terrified." He placed a hand on his chest. "And I think my heart might have stopped for a minute there. I guess it's about what I expected, to be honest."

The waitress stepped up. "Hi there, Alan. Can I freshen your coffee. Sorry, coffees?"

"Sure, if... did you just call me Alan?"

"That's your name, isn't it?"

"Yeah, but... well, it seems like folks tend to have a hard time remembering me."

"No offense, but," she gestured to her face, vaguely where Alan's injuries were, "you're kind of tough to forget."

He smirked, oddly proud.

"Well, Honey? Yes. Freshen my coffees. Both of them, please," he said. "We've got a big job ahead of us."

From The Author

Thank you for reading! If you liked this story, or perhaps if you found it lacking, I'd love to hear from you. You can find me online at my website, bookofdeacon.com. For **free stories** and important updates, join my newsletter.

Discover other titles by Joseph R. Lallo

The Book of Deacon – an Epic Fantasy Series:

Book 1: *The Book of Deacon*

Book 2: *The Great Convergence*

Book 3: *The Battle of Verril*

Book 4: *The D'Karon Apprentice*

Book 5: *The Crescents*

Book 6: *The Coin of Kenvard*

Book of Deacon Anthology: Volume 1

Book of Deacon Anthology: Volume 2

Other stories in the same setting:

The Rise of the Red Shadow

The Story of Sorrel

Entwell Origins: Anya

The Redemption of Desmeres

The Adventures of Rustle and Eddy

Jade

Halifax

The Stump and the Spire

The Big Sigma Series – a Sci-fi/Space Opera Series:

Book 1: *Bypass Gemini*

Book 2: *Unstable Prototypes*

Book 3: *Artificial Evolution*

Book 4: *Temporal Contingency*

Book 5: *Indra Station*

Book 6: *Nova Igniter*

Book 7: *Quantum Shift*

Beta Testers

Big Sigma Collection: Volume 1

Big Sigma Collection: Volume 2

The Free-Wrench – Steampunk Adventure Series:

Book 1: *Free-Wrench*

Book 2: *Skykeep*

Book 3: *Ichor Well*

Book 4: *The Calderan Problem*

Book 5: *Cipher Hill*

Book 6: *Contaminant Six*